Vigilante Marshal

When the second necktie-party went ahead right under the nose of US Marshal Bronco Madigan, he decided enough was enough. The first had him beat hands down, but the second victim was a man who had once saved his life. Conscious of the great debt he owed to that man, Madigan was prepared to walk up to the doors of Hell itself and kick them in to find those responsible.

Naturally, the outlaws were ready for him, and now his life was in danger. But Madigan was a tough hombre and the bad guys would be gambling with their fate.

Would Madigan get them before he was sent to Boot Hill?

DO'

Vigilante Marshal

TYLER HATCH

A Black Horse Western

ROBERT HALE · LONDON

Typeset by
Derek Doyle & Associates, Liverpool.
Printed and bound in Great Britain by
Antony Rowe Limited, Wiltshire

1
War Party

The Cheyenne war party kept Madigan pinned down in the buffalo wallow for two days. He hadn't slept in all that time, nor for the ten hours before the band of screaming warriors had come thundering over the rise, shooting their old rifles and hunting bows.

Two arrows had found homes in his racing mount and it had started to go down in a hurry as the wallow fell away beneath its faltering hooves. Dazed from the fall, dust choking him, Madigan had his rifle out and working before the horse had quit skidding, its weight actually carrying him deeper into the hollow.

The first two Cheyennes to top the rise went to meet their Great Spirit so fast neither one had time to even cry out the first notes of his Death Song. That gave the others pause and several started to haul their ponies aside. Madigan levered and fired as fast as he could to hurry them along. An arrow broke against the saddle-horn in front of his face as he sprawled between the vaguely twitching legs of the dying horse. He slid back and, when he cautiously raised his head again, there were no Indians to be seen. He used one more bullet to put the horse out of its final misery and reloaded the hot Winchester.

The Great Plains' sun burned down out of a blue furnace sky, beating through his worn shirt, making the sweat jump from his lean body. He was trail-dirty and beard-shagged and almighty weary. He started to curse the luck that had put him within arrow-shot of these hot-bloods, out for the scalp of a lone white man, but saved his breath. He untangled his canteen from the saddlehorn and shook it.

He already knew it was only half-full. It was a long way between waterholes out here and he had been closing on the next one he knew about. He decided to take one long, deep swallow because he had been sweating so much the dampness had dried into salt-scum on his clothes: he should've played safe and kept the extra water.

The Indians topped the rim again, spread out in a line. He counted eight.

But his mind told him that there had been at least four more trying to crowd their way out of the hollow after he had blasted them back. So, he needed to grow eyes in the back of his head, it seemed.

He slid down lower as the arrows and bullets thudded into the dead horse, shaking the carcass, but he only put the rifle over the already bloating belly and triggered three unaimed shots. Madigan knew the missing warriors would be coming from behind. He levered a shell into the smoking breech, hearing the warriors scatter, knew it was time for the others to make their appearance. He slid the Colt from its holster and laid it on the ground beside him as he belly-flopped around, facing the rear rim of the wallow.

Here they came! Wriggling across like four red, painted snakes, and these boys all had rifles, at least two Henrys, maybe one Leman trade rifle – which he discounted as being of no immediate danger. The other could be anything.

By that time he had started shooting, emptying the magazine, walking his shots along the writhing line, hearing two wail part of a Death Song, saw one drop his rifle – the trade gun, he thought – and the fourth leapt up and went hightailing back to the rim, the ends of his breechclout flying. Madigan deliberately put his last shot through the man's buttocks and grinned tightly at the howl of agony as the man stumbled and dragged himself out of sight. That left the one who had dropped his gun.

The man was braver than his comrades. He jumped up and, with hunting knife raised, cut loose with a chilling war-cry and hurled himself down in a flying leap. Madigan dropped the empty Winchester, spun on to his back even as he scooped up the sixgun. The Indian's body dropped upon him like a falling horse, jamming the gun hard in between them. Madigan grunted as the blade sliced into his left shoulder muscle, felt the flesh rip brutally as the Cheyenne tore the knife loose so he could try again.

Madigan didn't know which way the Colt was pointing, his hand was so numb and jammed so tightly. But he triggered anyway and yelled as the muzzle flash seared his belly and he immediately smelled smouldering cloth. The Indian's body jerked and started to fall away. Madigan fired again, kicked free, slapped at his smouldering shirt front with his left hand and swiftly rose to one knee, turning as he heard the rest coming back over the other rim.

He shot deliberately, ignoring the arrows that zipped past him and the *thuuuup!* of bullets. Two Indians toppled from their ponies, hit the slope and rolled and lay still. Another jerked upright, dropped his bow, clawed at his chest but managed to grip the mustang's flying mane and turn it back over the rim. The rest hauled on their hackamores and started to scatter. Madigan yelled insanely, triggering his empty gun before sagging back to his knees, panting, ears ringing, coughing in the dust and powdersmoke that hung thickly in the hollow like a dirty fog.

Shaking, his torn arm bleeding badly, he reloaded his weapons first, then tore off his neckerchief and bound up the arm. He saw the wound was going to give him trouble: an Indian hunting knife carried almost as many germs on the blade as a carrion-eater did between its teeth.

'This looks like it's going to be a right interesting couple of days,' he muttered, and swilled his mouth out with a little water. A *very* little. . . .

He shook the canteen again.

Yeah . . . gonna be mighty interesting. . . .

Ammunition, of course, soon became a worry – his

main concern after the lack of water. Food was OK for now – he still had a little hardtack left in the saddle-bag. But he knew that if he could survive for a day or so he would need to keep that in case he saw a way out and could make a run for it on foot. At the moment, it seemed the same as suicide to even contemplate escape on foot, but unless he learned to fly it was either that or let them bury him here.

Except that Indians didn't bury their white victims.

In any case, he took his knife and cut several steaks from the rump of the horse before it could spoil. He ate the meat raw from time to time while the Cheyenne stayed back, figuring out their strategy; once in a while one showing himself and shouting insults in his own lingo, trying to draw fire. They were smart enough to know ammunition would be his big problem as long as they could hold him besieged.

And water.

He tried to drink some of the horse's blood, but it made him sick. So it looked like he had to dole out his last mouthfuls of water in drops. Although the red meat contained juices, they were salty and only thickened his saliva, increasing his thirst.

He had likely been in tougher jams, but he couldn't think of any right now as he waited for the sun to set – and the night to bring whatever the Cheyenne had planned.

He knew they wouldn't like the idea of a night attack, but they wouldn't be afraid to try one. All he could do was wait. *And wait . . . and wait.*

And they kept him awake with screams and whoops

and the occasional gunshot and, in the midst of one of these sessions, a small group tried to get him from behind again. He was ready, shot three, although two dragged themselves back over the rim, clubbed one man's brains out with the brass butt of the rifle, and half-strangled yet another with the reins of the horse.

They retreated, dragging their dead, the wounded making their own way. If they couldn't that would be just too bad. . . .

The rest of the night they left him alone, but the constant yelling kept him awake. Which was probably just as well, anyway.

The next day they kept coming back to taunt him, trying to draw his fire. There was one small 'attack' by two young braves who were obviously only out to prove their manhood. They came roaring in in a blind charge on their wild-eyed mustangs, one with a bow and arrow, the other with a lance. He shot one, clubbed the other off the pony which shrilled wildly as it fell over his own dead mount. The other mustang ran off. Madigan draped the two men across the pony and sent the animal back out of the hollow.

He didn't aim to try to ground-hitch a half-wild pony in this cramped space, and he knew he couldn't ride the animal because his wounded shoulder was all swollen and festered, leaking pus, making his left arm all but useless. It hurt like hell to use his left hand to push home the last of his cartridges into the rifle's tubular magazine.

The fever was coming, he knew. There were flashes of brilliant, pale-yellow light at first, whirling bright dots behind his eyes. His thirst was monumental and there was no way to relieve it. He couldn't swallow the jerky, wasn't making enough saliva to moisten it sufficiently to get it down his gullet.

The Indians would know how he was – just because he hadn't seen them didn't mean they weren't there. He was puzzled as to why they were spending so much time on him. He had killed at least half of the war-party, wounded others. Many Indians would give up after that. They usually weren't out for glory – and what glory was there in a whole war-party killing a lone white man, anyway? They should have ridden off long since, and left him to die of thirst or the knife wound. He didn't even have a pack horse carrying goods that might have interested them. Not that their reasons mattered: he would end up just as dead.

Around mid-afternoon, he tightened his grip on the rifle, wincing as pain ran up his swollen left arm: he had slit the sleeve because the swelling was so bad. There was the sound of a horse climbing the rise beyond the rim. A lone horse.

It appeared bit by bit, ears first, then the head, chest, forelegs . . . he rose up slightly, blinking in an effort to clear his fever-dulled vision, looking for the rider. Then the man sat up from where he had been stretched out along the pony's back. He wore a head-dress, held a short lance in one hand, a rifle in the other. One half of his face was painted with a black star. He held his rifle high.

'We come for you, white man! Soon.'

Then the whole rim was lined with warriors, three

being men Madigan had wounded. They all held rifles except one man who had his bow already drawn on an arrow.

Madigan shook his head, blinking again, fumbling with the rifle, wishing he'd had enough bullets to fully load the sixgun as it would be easier to handle than the rifle with his swollen hand and arm.

But there was no time for regrets. This was to be Madigan's Last Stand, he figured, and the best he could do was to go down fighting, take as many of these Cheyenne with him as he could. Thing was he was too damn weary to care, too weary, too far gone in fever. Already he felt himself drifting away into unreality.

God! That meant they would riddle him, tear off his scalp, mutilate him . . . well, hell, what would it matter? He wouldn't know anything about it.

They were already halfway down the slope into the wallow, screaming and shooting, the bullets that penetrated the putrefying carcass of his horse releasing nauseous gases. He rolled away from its protection, cried aloud as his weight fell on his wounded shoulder.

The pain made his head whirl, but it also brought him rearing up in one final, savage defence, the butt of the rifle braced into his hip, blazing at the terrifying figures that filled his hazy vision.

He dropped the empty rifle, palmed up the sixgun, wishing he could remember how many shots remained. Maybe he ought to keep the last for himself. . . .

The din was ear-shattering, like something living, smashing into him with palpable force. Then he blinked as he swayed, seeing, unbelievably, the Indians who were still a'horse, turning to meet a new threat. *To them!*

A lone rider.

For an instant his vision cleared and he saw a man who looked to be in little better shape than himself, sitting a dusty, foam-caked horse, hatless, longish red hair catching the sunlight as he stood in the stirrups, a shotgun at his shoulder, thundering from both barrels. He discarded this as horses and Indians tumbled and scattered. Then he unsheathed a rifle, blazing away as fast as he could work the lever.

Madigan began to laugh, swaying, dropping to one knee. He fired his Colt, didn't see where the bullet went. The gun clicked empty as the Indians swept past him up and out of the wallow, pursued by the demon lone rider, still shooting the big Winchester with deadly results.

Then. . . .

Madigan couldn't believe it as the man abruptly jerked and twisted violently before spilling from the saddle, his suddenly limp body flying through the air towards Madigan himself. Madigan tried to dodge, but he was too slow and his rescuer's body smashed into him, pinning him to the ground with its dead weight. Streaks of light slashed his vision and a loud buzzing in his head suddenly faded into nothing. . . .

When he opened his eyes slowly, he groaned quietly, involuntarily, perhaps some deep instinct warning him not to make any more noise than he had to. He blinked in hot sunshine and then the sun was blotted out by a dark shape and he groaned again – louder this time.

He could make out the silhouette of an Indian, a man with a short lance and, as he turned his head slightly, a black star painted on one side of his face.

God, why couldn't you have let me stay dead! Now they'll torture what little life's left in me until they've had enough amusement and then just ride off and let me sample Hell before I finally cash-in.

Those were his fevered thoughts and then the lance came down towards him and he tensed, preparing himself for the stabbing pain of the flint point. The weight of the other white man still pinned his lower body to the ground.

Then there was a rough prodding at his upper chest and he winced as the pain transferred to his shoulder. But there was no slicing or tearing of his flesh by the flint spearhead.

The Cheyenne leaned down from the pony, looking into Madigan's pain-ravaged face.

'You fight well, white man. You send back young braves for burial . . . I count coup on you.'

It wasn't a short lance at all! It was a coup *stick! A goddamn coup stick!*

So that was why they'd persevered. He'd sent back the bodies of those two brash young warriors so they would be buried in the Indian way. And he had put up a good fight . . . now they didn't want to kill him.

Like many Indians, this one was acknowledging Madigan's bravery, content to let him live, content just to have touched his adversary with his coup stick.

'We meet again.' Then Black Star wheeled his mount

and walked it up out of the wallow. 'The day you die.'

Madigan didn't know which way he went and was past caring anyway.

Oblivion shot through with nightmares had already claimed him.

A finger of the white man pinning Madigan's legs twitched slightly. Once – twice – a pause – once more.

Then both bodies were stilled.

2
Nightmare

It was all a mixture of pain and nightmare, jumbled thoughts thundering around inside his throbbing head, the sweat streaming from his body. Cold steel sliced his flesh. Blood flowed.

'Don't take my arm, you son of a bitch!'

No answer. Just more pain. That damn Cheyenne with the black star painted on his face was grinning as he poked at him with his coup stick. Only it wasn't a coup stick at all – this time it was a lance with a razor-sharp spearhead and it stabbed and prodded at his body until he convulsed in pain.

'I come back, white man!'

That was the Cheyenne's parting shot.

'You do and I'll blow your damn head off!'

That was Madigan's rejoinder – only, afterwards, he couldn't be sure if he had actually said the words or only thought he did.

He was out on the Great Plains again, the sun

hammering at his pain-racked body, a strange horse moving under him, something heavy across his legs. He tried to see what it was, but couldn't bend his neck forward: it was too painful, felt stiff and swollen.

Mile after mile after mile. . . .

A rainstorm nearly did for him and the horse once in what had been a dry wash. A chocolate torrent came thundering down, washing small saplings and brush and gravel with it. He had no control: it was the horse that saved them.

Must be a cowpony, he thought.

The animal went with the flow until it shallowed and he could get a footing, heaved up out of the wash on to the muddy land, found a tree and rested. Madigan didn't know for how long.

More sun, more empty country. Leastways, what he could see of it, reeling around in the saddle as he did, eyes jerking in hot sockets, tongue swollen with thirst, body burning with fever and the intolerable throbbing pain in his left arm and side.

And still that weight across his thighs.

He felt gingerly with his right hand, but his brain was too fevered to tell him what he touched. Didn't matter. Had to keep going that was the thing. Keep – going – keep on. . . .

How the hell did he get to Parminter's office? For God's sake, that was in Washington!

But here he was, sitting in the visitor's chair that faced the big carved desk set across a large window whose glare effectively kept him from reading the chief marshal's face. A smart strategy, but Madigan always

figured it showed a chink in the armour of Federal
Marshal Miles Parminter. Showed he wasn't *quite* as
confident as he would have you believe.

'Bren. . . .' Parminter refused to call him by the nick-
name Madigan used when on assignment, *Bronco*,
preferred to call him by his given name. 'Bren, this time
you're going to Montana, place called Sky Creek.'

'Never heard of it.'

He thought Parminter had frowned but once again
that damn glare kept him from being sure. Madigan got
mild enjoyment out of annoying his chief by minor
interruptions and often wondered just what that said
about his own emotional make-up.

'Between the Powder River and Medicine Rocks in
the south-east corner,' Parminter told him in clipped
tones. 'Custer County.'

Madigan sighed. 'We're never gonna be able to
forget that madman, they keep tagging his name on
places all over the country.'

'Hero to some' the marshal said, this time slowly and
carefully, and Madigan could see by reflected light that
the man's lips had thinned-out beneath the silver
clipped moustache.

Time to quit the needling.

He merely nodded and the marshal took a cigarillo
from his engraved silver humidor and lit up before
continuing. He didn't offer one to Madigan which told
him he was being put in his place. He rolled a cigarette
as his chief told him his assignment. There had been a
lynching in the town of Sky Creek. There had been
rumours of a gold find and riff-raff had swarmed in

from all over the north, turning the countryside around the town into a pock-marked battlefield – with little to show for it, although there had been a few large nuggets located. That's all it took to perpetuate the wild dream of untold and easy-come riches, of course.

Law went out the window with the first strike and the army was too busy slaughtering Indians in retaliation for their victory over Custer, so things got out of hand. Gunfights in the street. Claim-jumping. Cold-blooded murder. Masked vigilantes prowling the town and the camps surrounding it, supposedly keeping law and order of a kind, but mostly robbing and finding excuses to kill men who were hitting paydirt.

Then there was a particularly brutal murder, a miner and his family slaughtered for a small poke of gold dust. There was real outrage and the vigilantes went berserk, storming through the camps, grabbing anyone they thought might know something. Eventually they pinned the killings on a man named Baxter, a newcomer, who had been befriended by the murdered family, taken in by them, given a bed and food.

This was what had incensed the miners: repaying kindness with theft and murder. . . .

Baxter was a rough man and had been in trouble in two of the whorehouses because of his handling of the women. The vigilantes tossed him into a cell, aiming to make an example out of him, put on a big trial, and enhance their own reputation for 'fair dealing'.

With bellies sloshing with rotgut that would scour the digestive tract of a grizzly, a mob had gathered and before morning, Baxter was swinging from a tall tree at the edge of town, guarded by masked men with guns to make sure the body stayed there, swinging in the breeze until it rotted. . . .

'Where do we come in, Chief?' Madigan asked. 'Local law could handle a lynching.'

He caught a glimpse of Parminter's eyes glinting at him. 'Baxter was a mining engineer, not a prospector – oh, he had done plenty of it before becoming an engineer. The Department of Mines sent him in to check out the real potential or otherwise of the gold-bearing area. There's never been too much gold found in Montana and if this was really a large reef, then the department wanted it managed properly and would have moved in if Baxter's report had shown it to be a major goldstrike.'

Madigan frowned. 'Just because he was undercover doesn't mean he *couldn't*'ve killed that miner and his family.'

'Of course not. That's what you have to find out and, naturally, bring the ring-leaders of that lynch mob to heel. Also, we don't tolerate vigilantes as you know.'

'Always some in a gold-rush town, Chief, but I'll find 'em and throw a scare into 'em.'

'You'll do more than that. If, as rumour has it, they've been using their vigilante activities as a cover for theft and murder, you'll bring them in and they'll find out what the inside of a Federal prison looks like.'

So Madigan outfitted and moved out to Sky Creek, Montana.

Everything blew up in his face. Someone had talked, and they knew who he was as soon as he arrived and there were several attempts on his life. Too bad that none of the would-be killers survived to give him any useful information. After that he was left alone for a spell, but he knew he was being dogged as he carried out his enquiries.

What he uncovered was a persistent rumour that the day after Baxter's lynching, two of the vigilantes found a crazy man living in a cave above the place where the miner and his family were slaughtered. They found body parts in various stages of being cooked and human bones from previous feasts staged by the loco old mountain man.

He was killed out of hand and the cave blasted-in and sealed forever. Baxter's body was cut down and buried in an unmarked grave in the over-crowded Sky Creek Boot Hill.

The whole town closed Madigan out more completely than ever. He had fights and they tried to kill him twice more, but he found out not a single thing. The vigilantes apparently disbanded voluntarily and he didn't even have the satisfaction of being able to name them.

It was one of the biggest failures of his career.

He wired a brief, undetailed report to Parminter, adding at the bottom of the message,

RETURNING BY HORSEBACK. TAKING MONTH'S LEAVE LONG OVERDUE. MADIGAN

No 'by your leave' or 'official request following', just a plain, bald statement: he was coming home the long way in an effort to come to terms with his failure.

It wasn't the first case he had lost, but it was the worst in Madigan's book. There was no peace or public vindication for Baxter's family; the vigilantes had got away with their own brand of law and order. He had sent a few villains to their Happy Hunting Grounds, but they had all been trying to kill him at the time. He had no sense of having accomplished a single worthwhile thing and that was a new sensation for Bronco Madigan, star undercover operative of the US Marshal's Office.

Maybe he was just getting old, he thought. Well, to hell with it. He had always liked Wyoming, despite the bitter winters, and he aimed to take his time crossing the Territory, enjoying a little hunting and living off the benevolent land, easing away all the tensions that had built up during the time spent in Sky Creek. There were a *lot* of frustrations to rid himself of.

That was the plan, anyway, but it went awry when that Cheyenne war party had come barrelling-in and trapped him in the buffalo wallow out on the Great Plains. . . .

He wondered who was the man who had saved his neck? Poor devil. Badly wounded with an arrow in the lower gut and a couple of bullets in a leg, plus a scalp-crease. . . .

Then the lucid time was over and he fell back into the sweat and nightmares of the fever.

Violent pictures from his past, and a few more pleasant ones, like Carrie Parker and her scarred body from that son-of-a-bitch of a brother of hers, Race Craddock.

For a time there he had thought he might be able to

help Carrie back along the road to rehabilitation, but Willis Matthews had come out from behind the façade of outlaw Barton McCall and now she was Carrie Matthews, and, last he had heard, there were two little Matthews running around . . . yeah, that was a pleasant thing to think about.

But there had been heaps more violence in Brendon Madigan's life than pleasantness and the nightmares took over and had him writhing and muttering and cursing, and then his own shouts mingled with the other sounds of fury – distant gunshots; men's voices, rough and edged with anger, shouting into the night; the crash of glass; the splintering of wood.

'*I got the rope! And, plenty of it!*'

A hoarse, excited voice, close by, he thought. *Damnit! He didn't want to think about that lynching!*

But the sounds, instead of fading, seemed to grow closer and his body trembled and shook with the scraping thunder of a hundred boots. Furniture was overturned. There was a garble of cursing, yelling voices.

Someone screamed, a weak, terror-driven sound, yet it penetrated to the deepest parts of Madigan's mind and his head seemed to explode. He smelled sweat.

'*Make sure he's out of it!*' someone said, and an instant later there was an overpowering sweetish smell, a burning sensation around mouth and nose and once more he plunged away into spiralling darkness, his nightmare over at last. . . .

When he warily opened his eyes this time, Madigan knew something had changed. His fever had broken!

He felt different, more *here* – wherever 'here' was.

He started to feel around with his hands. No, with his *right* hand. His left wouldn't move because it was firmly strapped across his chest with bandages. But there was pain and a burning heaviness in his left shoulder and down most of that side of his body. He felt sheets and tried to look down in the dim light, saw the end of a narrow bed, the shapes of other beds in a long room. There was movement at the far end.

Two men and a woman were setting a bed into place, apparently having moved it from somewhere else. The woman started to strip it and remake it with fresh sheets and pillow cases. Then one of the men went around opening drapes and sunlight streamed in through dusty windows.

He was a fairly big man in a collarless shirt and worn trousers. His heavy boots thudded on the floorboards of the room and he jumped when he saw Madigan staring at him with his sunken eyes.

'Judas! Sel – this feller's awake!'

The woman froze as she was tucking in a sheet. The other man, lean, and adjusting a battered hat, snapped his head around, glanced at Madigan.

'I'll fetch the doctor,' the woman said and hurried out.

The two men stood at the end of Madigan's bed, staring at him in silence, and then a tired-looking man with uncombed greying hair and rough white eyebrows came in, slipping suspenders over his shoulders. He pushed past the men and paused long enough to jerk his head towards the door and, somewhat reluctantly,

Madigan thought, they turned and left. But the one called Sel paused to give him a hard stare first.

The doctor had taken Madigan's pulse, looked into his eyes, did something with a bandage on his left shoulder that made Madigan gasp.

'Easy, Doc!' he rasped.

'I'll be easy,' the medic said a little testily. 'You have a drain in this wound. I'm just checking the wick. . . . Hmmm. Virtually clean. Another day and the wound will start healing quite quickly. You're a very lucky man, Mr Madigan.'

'You know my name?'

The doctor's narrow, lined face broke into a half smile as he held a glass of water against Madigan's parched lips. 'Not too much too fast, man! Easy does it – sip slowly. Yes, you had some papers.'

Madigan grunted, his eyes following that cool glass of water as the doctor set it down on a small bedside table. 'Where am I?'

'Nightowl Creek, Wyoming. I'm Dr Tucker and this is my infirmary in town. You rode in three days ago. Quite the worse for wear.'

Suddenly remembering the weight that had been across his thighs as the horse took him across the Great Plains, Madigan asked, 'What happened to the feller who was with me?'

Doctor Tucker went very still, looking down at Madigan soberly.

'I'm afraid he didn't – survive, Mr Madigan. He died last night.'

3
Boot Hill

Madigan studied the doctor as the man ran his hand through his long grey hair. It seemed to be shaking slightly.

'Those wounds finish him?' Madigan asked.

The doctor hesitated, then nodded. 'Yes, I suppose they did . . . I mean by that, that I had to amputate his leg and – well, the arrow head in his stomach had done considerable internal damage. . . .' He paused, cleared his throat, shook his head. 'He was a mess. Must've been tough to survive that ride in across your lap.'

Madigan nodded. 'Can't recall much about that. Damn Indian with a black star painted on his face counted coup on me and I passed out. He must've left the other feller's mount because mine was long dead.'

'I see.'

'Know who he was?'

The doctor looked up sharply. 'I – no. Just some drifter playing at being a Good Samaritan, I suppose.'

Madigan frowned and his voice, although weaker than usual, had a hard edge. 'Doc, that "drifter" *was* a Good Samaritan – he saved my life!'

'Yes, yes, of course, I didn't mean any kind of slur on the man. Look, I'll have my wife bring you some food and we'll get that wound cleaned up and redressed. You should be ready to leave in a day or so.'

Madigan was surprised to find that the doctor's wife was the young woman who had been remaking the bed at the far end of the infirmary when he had come to – with the help of the two hardcases. She must have been more than twenty years the medic's junior. She was pleasant, said her name was Marion as she set a bed-tray across his lap. There were dishes of scrambled eggs, some sort of fried sausage, fried-over potatoes and thick toasted bread as well as a small pot of coffee.

'I don't know how hungry you feel, but – just eat what you want to. I won't be offended if you leave something.'

He answered her smile faintly. 'Looks good, ma'am, and I thank you.' As she turned to leave he asked, 'Those two fellers who were helping you with the bed. . . .'

She turned sharply, her tall figure stiffening, he thought. The smile had gone now. 'Yes?' Curtly spoken.

'They looked kinda tough to be working in a place like this.'

For a moment she remained sober then she laughed shortly. 'Oh, my, *yes!* They are indeed! Sel Carnaby and Billy-Jack Reed. They do odd jobs around town, sometimes hire out as deputies when the sheriff needs them

. . . don't worry, I doubt you'll see them again in here.'

She left and the ring of her gentle laughter remained in the air, but Madigan noticed she seemed glad to get away from his presence.

He dozed after the meal and needed the lavatory when he woke again. He was the only patient and he was damned if he was going to call Marion, so he eased himself out of bed and stood experimentally. The room swayed some and his shoulder hurt but, barefoot and a little unsteadily, he groped his way down the line of beds towards the narrow door marked 'Lavatory'.

He cursed and snatched the iron frame of the last bed in line, reaching down too fast so that he flopped on to the bed itself. Then he lifted his left foot and pulled a sliver of glass from the meaty pad behind his large toe. The wound bled only a little but it had sure given him a jab. He put the sliver on the bedside table, noticing how it swayed on its legs, saw one joint splintered at a corner. The wood showing through the layer of old varnish was white and fresh-looking.

Puzzled, he eased himself down on to one knee and found more broken glass beneath the bed. Brown glass, as if from a medicine bottle, and some thin clear curved glass like from the chimney of a lamp.

The rest of the infirmary was immaculate. Seemed strange that this corner was so sloppy. Then again, maybe they'd had a violent patient in the bed or one of those clumsy hardcases could have knocked over the table.

Hell, what did it matter? He needed the lavatory. . . .

*

After his wound had been cleaned and bandaged, the doctor told him it should heal swiftly.

'Suppose you'll want to be moving along to wherever you were going when the war party attacked you?'

'No real hurry, Doc. That feller who helped me – where'd they bury him?'

Why the hell did that question seem to shake up the medic? Judas, the man jumped as if he had been jabbed with a cactus on the bare butt.

'Er – Boot Hill, where else?'

Madigan tried to hold the man's gaze but the other busied himself picking up his scissors and needles and lotions. 'Like to see his grave, Doc.'

'Well, that's – understandable. Suppose we leave that till tomorrow morning, though? The sheriff will be back in town by then and he'll want to interview you anyway. . . .'

Passing the buck, thought Madigan, but agreed that tomorrow would be fine.

They left him pretty much alone for the rest of the day. He got out of bed twice, took short walks around the long room, looked at the town through the dusty windows.

Not much of a place, all timber except for a brick building he figured could be the bank, and another whose front was adobe. He could just make out the lettering on the weathered wooden sign swinging from rusty chains above the door: LAW OFFICE – *Sheriff Jackson Quinn.*

Madigan had never heard of the man. He watched from time to time, but didn't see anyone go into or come out of the law office until just before sundown when the two hardcases, Carnaby and Reed, entered. He heard Marion bringing his evening meal and hobbled back to bed. She was as pleasant as ever but he still felt there was some uneasiness in her. He asked if she could bring him some writing paper and a pen and a long envelope. She complied with a smile and while he waited he started to eat.

It was a fine meal and he was hungry.

Chief Marshal Parminter picked up the silver handbell off his desk and rang it peremptorily. When the door from the outer office didn't open immediately, he kept shaking the bell until a breathless clerk came hurrying in.

'Sorry, Marshal – belly's playin'-up again today.'

Not so much as a grunt of sympathy or acknowledgement from Parminter.

'Any further word from Madigan?'

'No, sir. Only that wire to say he was takin' a month's leave.'

Parminter's mouth tightened beneath his moustache. He tapped thick fingers on some papers on his desk. 'He knows better than to pull that kind of stunt.'

The clerk shifted uneasily. 'Well, sir, it's not usual for Marshal Madigan to fail – I'd say he's tryin' to come to terms with it.'

'Oh, that's what you'd say is it? Well, I have a deskful of work here and I need every man in the field I can lay my hands on! He hasn't even had the courtesy to send in an interim report. Send a wire to all field operatives that they're to keep an eye out for him and to tell him to get in touch with me *immediately!*'

'Yessir!'

The clerk was glad to get out of there.

Jackson Quinn was a largish man with a hardy protruding belly and a pendulous underlip. He was a man in his late forties or early fifties and he either thought he was tough or he *was* tough: that part had yet to be proved to Madigan's satisfaction.

He walked slowly to match Madigan's steps at first, but soon grew tired of it and strode out ahead. Folk on the street nodded to him or said 'Howdy, Jackson,' and most gave Madigan a look that was strangely curious and, in a couple of cases, openly hostile. He was still a little weak after leaving his sickbed, but he had the nagging feeling that Doc Tucker was kind of glad to be rid of him. The sheriff seemed satisfied with his story although he kept returning to the stranger who had saved Madigan's life, kept asking if Madigan was *sure* the man hadn't identified himself.

'Listen, you take your time,' the lawman called back along the boardwalk and turned to point to a grey rise at the north end of town. 'Boot Hill's up there. You wander on up and I'll join you soon.'

Madigan slogged along, looking around the town and being no more impressed than when he had seen it through the dusty panes of the infirmary windows. There were empty, boarded-up shops, a lot of aban-

doned shacks and houses. It looked like a dying town to
him. He looked back once to see where the sheriff had
gone, but the big man had apparently ducked into the
livery stables or the general store for he was not visible
on the boardwalks.

The only other place he could have gone was the
small telegraph office, but Madigan could see through
the tiny window and there was no one in sight, not even
the operator.

A little way down the block there was the stage depot
and he looked once more to make sure Quinn hadn't
finished his business and was already overtaking him,
then turned in through the agency doors.

He took a bulky envelope from inside his shirt and
slipped it under the wire to the counter-clerk. 'I want
that to go on the stage to Cheyenne and then – *only*
then – I want it mailed to the address on the front.'

No sense in letting Parminter know exactly where he
was and the interim report he had written out might
keep him off his back a little longer.

The clerk, weary, past middle age as well as his prime,
mopped sweat from his bald dome, adjusted his
eyeshade and half-moon glasses, squinting at the
address, his lips moving slightly as he read. He snapped
up his head.

'Federal Marshal's Office! In Washington?'

'Can you do what I asked?' Madigan cut in impatiently and the man hesitated and nodded.

'Sure – no trouble.'

'Well, just in case you have to make an extra special
effort. . . .' Madigan pushed a silver dollar under the

wire. 'This is for you – and this' – he slid another five dollars across – 'for the shipping and mailing of the letter. Any change you keep, OK?'

The clerk smiled crookedly, pocketing the coins and slipping the envelope under the counter. 'I gotcha – I keep the change and my mouth shut, right?'

Madigan's bullet-like eyes disturbed the clerk as the undercover marshal nodded. 'That you better do most of all, friend.'

The man swallowed, assured Madigan he could keep a secret, and then Madigan left and made his weary way up to the gates of Boot Hill. The sheriff was leaning against a post, firing-up a cigarette.

'Thought you must've sprouted wings – you bookin' out on the stage?' The lawman seemed eager for him to say he was.

'Checking prices. Don't feel like I could fork a horse very far right now so might take the stage when I leave. Now where's the grave of this feller. . . ?'

The sheriff led the way to a far corner way at the back and Madigan slowed his pace. The lawman was frowning back at him when he arrived at the graveside.

'You must be feelin' more poorly than you look.'

'Why'd they bury him 'way back here? No marker even.'

Quinn shrugged. 'I was out of town, but I'd say because no one knew him and he had no money on him so they put him here.'

'In the paupers' section.'

Quinn's face was hard. 'Reckon he knows the difference?'

'He mightn't but I do – for Chris'sakes, Quinn, the man saved my life! Rode into a bunch of blood-crazy Indians and saved my hide. He deserves better'n this.'

Quinn shrugged. 'County funds won't run to better. But, if it really bothers you—'

'It does.'

'OK, you can have a headboard put up if you like. Guess you could even move him back to a decent part of the cemetery, but it'll be at your expense.'

'Fine with me.' Madigan shook his head, looking down at the trampled fresh earth. 'Looks like the whole damn town danced on the grave!'

The sheriff's look was both startled and narrow. 'The hell're you sayin', Madigan?'

'That's the way it looks to me.'

Quinn studied the trampled ground, frowning. 'Must've been the grave-diggers, for some reason – I'll check it out.'

'Wouldn't't've been Carnaby and Reed, would it?'

Jackson Quinn stiffened. His right hand seemed to want to edge towards his single holstered Colt but it stopped with a twitch before it got going properly. 'Who the hell are you, Madigan?'

'Doc said he – or someone – found what papers I was carrying. They'll tell you all you'll need to know.'

'Which ain't the same as sayin' as much as I'd *like* to know. There's somethin' different about you, Madigan . . . but this ain't gettin' us nowhere. You want me to, I'll have the body moved to a better part of the Hill and I'll take you to the undertaker for a headboard.'

'I want a head*stone* – there a stonemason in town?'

Quinn spread his hands. 'Sure – it's your money.'

'I figure my life's worth at least that much.'

'Guess you'd know. . . .'

The stonemason was a tubby man who smelled of sweat and marble dust and wore a stiff leather apron around his ample middle. His face was moon-like and pleasant. He watched the sheriff leave after introducing Madigan and telling the mason, McCann, what he wanted.

'Got some sandstone that polishes up nice, shows the grain and strata – cheaper than granite, too.'

'Price doesn't matter within reason, but I like sandstone, so make it that. I want the date he died and you can add something like – *Unknown to the man whose life he saved and who, in gratitude, erected this headstone.* You can fix the words to suit, I guess.'

'Judas, all that for Red—!' The stonemason stopped, looking up quickly from his notebook. 'I mean—'

Madigan moved in close. He only had one good arm but his big hand fisted-up the stiff leather apron and he pushed the man back against a half-finished sculpture of a life-size angel in blue granite and held him there roughly.

'*Red?* You know who he was?'

McCann was shaking his head wildly, eyes staring. 'No, no, but he had red hair and someone just labelled him "Red". All I meant was it seemed a pretty good inscription for a man you know nothin' about. I mean he could've been an outlaw, or a killer. . . .'

Madigan slowly released the man. 'Friend, I don't

care if he was the Devil's sidekick. All I know is he saved my life and I'm gonna see he's remembered for it.'

McCann gave an involuntary groan which he covered quickly and turned into a cough. 'I'll – see to it, mister. How soon you want it?'

'I guess I'll be quitting town in a few days so don't waste any time getting to it.'

McCann assured him he wouldn't and seemed mighty glad when Madigan left.

He called in at the church to ask the preacher if he would say a few words over the unknown hero when he was reinterred. It surprised the hell out of him when the clergyman, cadaverous, pious, and self-assured of his place in the Afterlife, shook his head so vigorously his jowls quivered.

'No! I cannot!' He saw Madigan's face, the puzzlement slowly fading to be replaced by rising anger. The preacher forced a death's-head smile and held up a bony hand.

'Please don't misunderstand, Mr Madigan! He was one of God's creatures and, of course, deserves to have the Bible read over his grave but I-I have been summoned to – to Cheyenne where a visiting pontiff has granted me an audience. It's an honour I simply can't afford to let pass, so I'm most terribly sorry, but I must decline your request.'

He squirmed under Madigan's stare. 'You leaving the town without a man of the cloth to keep them on the straight and narrow, preacher?'

The clergyman forced a brief laugh. 'Oh this is a God-fearing town, Mr Madigan. I have no worry that its inhabitants will transgress while I am absent! Now, if you'll excuse me. . . ?'

Madigan had more questions but decided to let it go.

The doctor was startled by Sheriff Quinn's hurried and noisy entrance to his office to one side of the infirmary.

The lawman looked grim.

'Doc, how soon's that Madigan gonna be fit to ride?'

'Why – two, perhaps three days . . . four at the most.'

Quinn swore. 'Make it two – *at the most!*'

The doctor paled. 'What – what's happened?'

'Relax – nothin' much but I'm playin' a hunch.'

'About what, Jackson?'

'Madigan.' Quinn's pale eyes narrowed, his mouth a razor slash. 'Yeah, I think the son of a bitch is some kinda lawman. I ain't usually wrong with my hunches. He asks a lot of damn sharp questions, right to the point, like he's used to it.'

'Like a lawman, you mean?'

'Yeah. So you get him outa town quick as you can, savvy? He starts pokin' around and we're all dead – or *he* is. And I'm here to tell you if he *is* the law it won't be no fun when they send someone to find out how he died.'

Doctor Tucker looked old and grey-faced. 'Oh, the *hell* with it, Jackson! What kind of warped fate made him bring Red Haskell *here* of all places on this earth!'

'Good question, Doc – and we better find an answer or we've got more trouble than you can shake a stick at.'

Doc Tucker was shaking now. 'It's all right for you, you arranged to be out of town when—'

The big sheriff moved in fast, crushing the medico against the wall. He breathed his bad breath into Tucker's frightened face. 'Just get him out of town! And *fast!*'

4
Mystery

It was some time during the early hours that Madigan awoke to hear urgent voices and scuffling sounds of effort in the dark end of the infirmary. Lamplight reflected through the doorway from the passage that led to Dr Tucker's residence and in its glow he could make out Marion Tucker, the doctor and Reed and Carnaby carrying a man between them. The man's arms dangled, fingers just trailing on the floor.

'Put him on the bed!' panted the doctor and Marion left the room hurriedly as her husband bent over the injured man.

'What's happened?' Madigan asked, struggling to prop himself up on his right arm.

The men all turned towards him.

'Go back to sleep, drifter,' growled Sel Carnaby. 'This is nothin' to do with you.'

But the doctor said, 'Sel and Billy-Jack found this man lying in an alley when they were on night patrol . . . he's been badly beaten, probably robbed.'

'Who is he?'

'Don't know for sure yet, but . . .' began the doctor, as his wife came back with a bowl of water and antiseptic and some cloths.

Billy-Jack Reed cut in, 'Take Sel's advice, mister, just go back to sleep.'

Madigan said nothing, remained propped on his good arm and watched the doctor work on the man on the bed, aided by Marion. Sel stood by, arms folded and Reed picked up a cloth, dipped it in the antiseptic and bathed the knuckles of his right hand, then his left.

Sel Carnaby came down to stand at the end of Madigan's bed. 'Get some sleep. You've got a long ride ahead of you, wouldn't wonder.'

'Why would you wonder that?'

'Understand from the Doc that you're about ready to leave.'

'Maybe yes, maybe no. I'll leave here whenever Doc says, but I may stick around town for a spell.'

'The hell would you do that for?'

'Got an interest here.'

Sel's face looked tight and angry. 'This town ain't got no interest in you, Madigan. I was you, I'd ride out, or take the first stage soon as Doc says you can travel.'

'Well, I'll play that card when it's dealt to me. You got a special interest in seeing me leave town?'

Carnaby scowled. 'I got no interest in you, or what you do, mister.'

Madigan smiled slowly.

'Glad to hear it.'

Sel looked puzzled.

'Saves us locking horns.'

Carnaby straightened. 'Listen, you damn saddle-tramp! I'm a duly-sworn night deputy, and if I say you do somethin', you jump and do it!'

'How about the daytime when you're not wearing that badge?'

Carnaby growled and moved around the bed, but Reed's sharp voice stopped him.

'Sel! Doc's busy here. We might's well finish the patrol and come back later, find out who this is. Come on, man!'

Carnaby went reluctantly and Madigan saw Marion's white face as she studied him. She turned back swiftly to the injured man when she saw him gazing at her. He swung his legs out of the bed and moved across. Doc Tucker glanced up uneasily.

'You should just leave this to us, Mr Madigan.'

'Christ! Beg your pardon, ma'am. Poor devil sure got a working-over. Wait! Isn't he the clerk from the stage depot?'

The Tuckers exchanged looks and Marion nodded. 'I believe it is Mel McConnell. He should know better than to stay out this late getting drunk.'

Tucker didn't like it when Madigan moved closer, picked up the table lamp that Marion had brought and held it closer to the raw meat that was McConnell's face. The man's clothes were filthy, torn, his body bruised, the shape of boots plain to see against the damaged flesh.

'He's been worked over by experts,' Madigan gritted. 'Seemed harmless enough when I saw him earlier at the depot. He a boozer?'

'No, not really,' Marion said, and then flushed as she caught her husband's eye.

Tucker cleared his throat and said, 'Not what you call a drunk, but if Mel has a spare dollar in his pocket he usually ties one on.'

He didn't sound convincing and probably knew it because he concentrated on sewing up some of the gashes in Mel's battered face.

'Didn't strike me as a man who'd be worth beating-up like this and robbing,' Madigan allowed.

'Well, I don't really know a lot about him,' Doc Tucker said crisply. 'He's usually healthy enough. I suppose I've only seen him as a patient five or six times in as many years.'

'Then he doesn't make a habit of getting into fights.'

Tucker's lips compressed. 'As I say, I don't know him that well . . . look, Mr Madigan, you can see how busy I am here, why don't you go back to bed? We'll try not to disturb you too much.'

'Couldn't get back to sleep now, Doc. Anyway, be daylight in an hour. Think I'll go for a stroll around town.'

The Tuckers didn't like that, but said nothing as Madigan picked up the piece of rag he had seen Reed use to dab antiseptic on his knuckles: it was smeared with blood. . . .

The morning was cool and there were one or two lights showing in buildings on Main. Madigan didn't see any sign of Reed or Carnaby as he stepped up onto the raised boardwalk outside the general store. A light burned in the back as the storekeeper and his family prepared for the day's trade. On a corner of the walk stood a barrel containing axe and pick handles of various sizes.

Madigan chose a hickory pick handle with a thick end and a smooth grip. He hefted it, and, satisfied, stepped down off the walk and then prowled the back streets and alleys searching for the night deputies.

Down behind the livery stables, he heard their voices as they sat on the bottom rail of the corral, smoking cigarettes and drinking from a flat pint bottle of rotgut. Reed suddenly cursed.

'Goddamn likker! Burns like acid.' He held up his left hand, shaking it. 'Split my knuckles on that damn clerk and whiskey just run down into the cuts.'

'Should've wrapped your hands in a neckerchief like I done.'

'I wanted the son of a bitch to feel it,' Reed growled and drained the bottle. He tossed it aside, stood up and belched. 'Might's well head for home, eh, Sel?'

'Might's well.'

They started towards the stables' main building where Madigan waited in the shadows. He pressed back against the wall, raising the pick handle. As they came opposite, chatting easily, he stepped out and swung the handle with all his force into Reed's big midriff. The man gagged and gave a strangled cry, leaping off the ground even as he doubled over and sprawled to hands and knees.

Carnaby jumped aside wildly, reaching for his gun but the hickory smashed into the side of his neck and almost tore his head off his shoulders. He moaned as he writhed about on the ground. Madigan walked across to where Reed was fighting for breath and kicked him savagely in the ribs. The man toppled over on to his side and Madigan kicked him twice more in the body, smashed the butt-end of the hickory handle down into Reed's contorted face. The nose crunched and teeth broke as lips mashed. Madigan kicked him once more in the belly for luck and turned to Carnaby who was barely conscious.

He whacked the handle across the man's back and heard the breath explode out of him. Carnaby convulsed and finished up on his back, staring dully up at the stars. Madigan broke his left collar bone, stomped on his belly and tossed the hickory handle far away into the weed-grown lot beyond the corrals.

He hadn't made a sound since delivering the first blow. He strolled back to the infirmary unhurriedly and the Tuckers seemed surprised to see him so soon.

'Town's not safe,' Madigan said, sitting on his bed and removing his boots. 'Helluva brawl of some kind down behind the livery – I never went to see, but there was a lot of yelling and moaning. You'll likely have more customers before daylight, Doc.'

He stretched out on top of the bed in his street clothes, hands locked behind his head, staring up at the ceiling.

There was a strangely satisfied look on his rugged face.

'Not much of a town, this, Doc,' he said. 'Looks like it's waiting for burial.'

Doc Tucker and Marion exchanged a strange glance – strange to Madigan, anyway – and the medic heaved a sigh and said, 'I'm afraid that's all too close to the mark, Mr Madigan. It used to be quite prosperous, a trail town. Then Kit O'Bannion opened the trail to Cheyenne through Laramie and we – well, deteriorated. People here don't walk with a swing in their step any longer, hardly any bother to smile. Some can't even be bothered to speak. No, we're a classic, dying town, Mr Madigan. Nowhere to go except down.'

'Isn't Union Pacific driving a railroad through this part of the country?'

'Further north. Going through the Medicine Bows via Saratoga Pass – which makes good sense, of course. But it certainly would put Nightowl Creek on the map again if they were to come through here.'

Madigan grunted. 'Well, I'm feeling tired now, Doc. Guess I'll catch a little shut-eye.'

'Good idea . . . rest is important to a swift recovery.'

The doctor and Marion left quietly.

Madigan waited a spell, then rolled off the bed and went to stand beside Mel McConnell's bed. The man wore a lot of bandages on both his head and body, one good eye watching Madigan warily.

'Sure worked you over, pard. Relax, Mel, I'm sorry this happened to you. I didn't pay you enough not to tell 'em what they wanted to know and that was my fault. But it's OK. Gospel. And I'll take care of your medical expenses.'

For a moment the eye merely stared, then it began to slowly fill with tears. Madigan gently squeezed his arm.

'Take it easy, Mel. They won't give you any more trouble.'

The single eye widened as Madigan moved away.

The stonemason was at work early by the sound of the chipping hammers as he entered the yard. But he saw it was McCann's protégé, Ernie, working. The youth looked sharply at Madigan

'Where's McCann?'

'Feelin' poorly – up to the house,' the youth said without looking up.

Madigan found the stonemason resting on the porch. His right hand was heavily bandaged and there were a few spots of blood showing. Madigan stopped at the foot of the short steps, his face grim.

'You have a visit from Reed and Carnaby last night?'

McCann nodded, looking sick. 'Bastards crushed my fingers with my own maul!'

'Why?'

McCann glared, his pudding-like face no longer appearing humorous. 'Because I was makin' that headstone for you! Said you wasn't to have anythin' done for you in this town. They smashed up what I'd already done on your stone. I'll give you back your money.'

'Forget it. Looks like someone wants me outa town in a hurry. ' He stepped up on to the porch and the mason looked anxious. 'McCann, why did you call that feller "Red"? And don't you say "which feller" or I'll—'

'Told you, because of his hair.'

'That's what you told me, yeah, but I want the real reason. You knew him, didn't you?' McCann shook his head vigorously, looking quite sick now as he swiftly denied it. 'Look, Reed and Carnaby are in Doc Tucker's infirmary and likely they'll be there for quite some time.'

'Wh-what happened?'

'Someone beat-up on 'em down behind the livery while they were on town patrol early this morning. Way they looked, I'd say whoever it was used a pick handle.'

'Judas!' McCann breathed and for a moment something like happiness flared in his eyes. 'By God, they've had that comin' for a long time!'

'Mel McConnell would agree with you – but never mind that. Let's get back to "Red". That feller was a stranger to me. He come riding in a'smokin' against at least six Cheyenne; I was out of ammo and had nowhere to go but to the Happy Hunting Grounds. He was badly wounded and I never even had a chance to exchange one word with him . . . when I came to in town he was dead. Now, I want to know who he was and I'm not leaving this dump until I find out. You want to help me?'

McCann remained silent and the inner struggle was plain on his face, but in the end, he shook his head slightly. He held up his bandaged hand.

'This is bad enough – I say any more and they'll kill me.'

Madigan could see the man's fear was genuine. 'All right. Just tell me this: did Red come from this town?'

The mason sucked in a sharp breath, chewed at his lower lip a spell then nodded jerkily, adding quickly, 'That's all I got to say! I mean it, Madigan, I'm too scared to say more.'

'OK, I'll settle for that as a starting point. Obliged, McCann. Set your man working on another stone for me.'

The mason's jaw dropped.

'Just do it. I guarantee you the sheriff'll agree.'

'The ... the sheriff? I never mentioned Jackson Quinn!'

'Didn't have to. They may think I'm some dumb saddletramp, but I'm not.'

Madigan nodded and stepped down to the yard, had taken several steps when McCann called hoarsely, 'He don't think you're just a drifter! He reckons you smell of law!'

Madigan smiled coldly and resumed his pace without looking around.

The town wasn't friendly to him: no credit anywhere. Luckily he had enough money left to wire the Marshals' Field Paymaster's Agency in Denver, although it wasn't called anything like that publicly. It went under a code name as a special section of the Colorado First National Bank. The request had all the outward appearance of being an advance against an account in the applicant's name. With any luck, there would be the cash in his name sitting at the local Wells Fargo branch in a day or two. Of course, a copy of the request would eventually filter through to Parminter's office and the man would know exactly where he was, but he had a little time.

And he aimed to use it to clear up this mystery about the man who had saved his life – and who had himself departed this life before Madigan had had a chance to thank him personally.

He was a man who hated to be beholden at any time, but something like this – well, he'd move hell and high-water and kick the devil's ass if he had to, but he would make sure this mystery-man Red was going to be remembered as a hero and honourably, no matter what his past might have been.

Anyone stupid enough to get in his way had better learn to side-step mighty quick or they could find them-selves six feet under the sod where they stood.

Not Wanted

The livery man, Bo Johansen – known to most Nightowl Creek folk simply as 'Swede' – was forking hay into a stall when Madigan came down the aisle. He was a long-armed, thick-wristed man with a horse-like face and stringy colourless hair that dangled irritatingly across one eye – irritatingly to others, that is. It didn't seem to bother Swede.

He never brushed it away from that left eye.

He saw Madigan coming and stiffened, then shook the fork's twin tines free of hay and rested the points on the floor between his big manure-covered boots. He looked at Madigan hostilely.

'What you want?'

'My saddle-bags.'

'Don't have 'em.'

'I recollect dragging 'em from under my horse in the buffalo wallow, slinging 'em across the cantle of the horse the Indians had left me. Someone in town's got 'em.'

'Not me.' Swede squinted. 'Ask the sheriff. An' why would a Cheyenne leave you a hoss to ride out? Why din' he kill you an' steal the hoss?'

His tone said that Madigan was lying and he wanted an explanation. Madigan smiled crookedly. 'Mister, you dunno Indians, I guess. He counted *coup* on me, said we'd meet again. That's their way. He didn't feel like killing me that time, next time he likely will. By the way, you want to buy that horse?'

Swede blinked. 'The one you rode in with . . . the other feller?' Madigan nodded and the big man shook his head. 'Not your hoss to sell.'

'Figure it is. Red saved my neck, and he died doing it. The Cheyenne left the horse for me. Reckon that makes it mine and I'm in need of some ready cash.'

The livery man's face coloured. 'Don't you try crowdin' me, mister! That hoss is mine, now. It belonged to Red Haskell and like you say now he's dead so. . . .'

The look on Madigan's face stopped the man in mid-sentence. 'So that was his name – Red Haskell.'

Swede's eyes widened and then narrowed. As Madigan took a step forward, he lifted the two-tined fork menacingly.

'Stay back! Or I'll skewer your other arm, too!'

'This one?' Madigan held up his good right arm and Swede's gaze instinctively swung to it. The marshal kicked out savagely and the big man grunted as he stumbled, almost fell.

Madigan stepped forward, kicked the man's legs out from under him and wrenched the fork from his grip, jabbing the handle up under Swede's lantern jaw. He reversed it by rolling it swiftly around his fingers like a drum-major's baton, stomped a boot into the middle of Swede's chest and held the tines either side of the livery-man's throat. Swede went very still his pale eyes flaring with fear, pinned by the neck. '*No!*' he croaked.

Madigan spoke softly. 'Tell me about Red Haskell.'

'I dunno no Red Haskell! That wasn't what I said.'

It ended in a scream as Madigan thrust forward and the tines dug into the ammonia-damp earth of the stall, the curve of the fork coming down firmly across Swede's throat, half-strangling him.

'Red Haskell!' Madigan gritted, leaning his weight on the fork.

Swede writhed.

'The hell you think you're doin'!'

Sheriff Jackson Quinn's angry voice came from behind Madigan and the marshal glanced over his shoulder, saw the sheriff had a sixgun in his hand. As he looked, Quinn cocked the hammer.

'Let him up! *Now!*'

Madigan withdrew the fork and held it in his one good hand, tines downward. Swede rolled away, clawing at his throat, hawking. Quinn kicked him brutally in the side.

'Get on your feet, you blabber-mouth bastard!'

Swede staggered up, plainly afraid of Quinn. 'Jackson, I never—'

'Where'd he get the name "Haskell" then? Aah – go wash-up you, dumb son of a bitch! Then come back and give Madigan a fair price for Red's hoss.'

'No, Jackson! That hoss is mine!'

When Quinn started towards him, Swede backed off and hurried away down the aisle. And when Quinn turned back he felt the fork's tines prick his midriff. He sucked in his big belly swiftly, rising to his toes.

'Don't be stupid, Madigan! You're in enough trouble as it is!'

'*You* tell me about Red Haskell – and why everyone says they don't know him.'

'I've got my Colt pointin' at your weddin'-tackle, friend! You might stick me, but you'll die a lingerin' death anyway.'

So Quinn was as tough as he looked, thought Madigan and he slowly lowered the fork, but held on to it, leaning on the handle.

'How come this town denies knowing a man who was a real-life hero? Buried him in a pauper's grave, smashed up the headstone I'd ordered. *And* beat the hell out of a stage-line clerk just because I gave him a letter to post.'

Quinn's eyes narrowed. 'Addressed to the US Marshal's Office in Washington ... if you're some kind of law, Madigan, you don't come sneakin' into my town by the back door and start upsettin' everyone in sight.'

'You want to know why I wrote to the Marshals? I was putting in a claim for a reward on a feller I tangled with up in Montana. Dandy Joe Cutter. Shot a marshal in Santa Fe couple years ago. Figured I might's well claim the bounty.'

Quinn thought it over, scowled. 'Shoulda done it

through me. You want to know *anythin'* in this town, you ask me.'

'Believe I did just that – out at Red Haskell's grave.'

'Yeah – well, I didn't know the details myself then. Told you, I'd had to go outa town the night he died.'

Madigan stiffened and his face was so ugly with rising fury at a thought that started to form in his head, that Quinn took an involuntary step backward.

'Just how did he die?'

'Didn't Doc Tucker tell you?'

'He said complications from the arrow wound in his gut and having his leg amputated.'

'That's right – complications. You can take that as gospel. And when Swede pays you for Red's old hoss, you can catch the next stage out.'

Madigan locked gazes with the sheriff. 'I don't think so.'

Jackson Quinn swore softly. 'You *are* a mule-headed son of a bitch, ain't you!'

'You ain't seen nothing yet, Quinn.'

The sheriff swore loud and long. 'What the hell is the matter with you? You know Red's name, how he died. I've made arrangements to have him reburied in a better part of the cemetery and I've fixed it for you to get some money ... and still you're bein' stubborn!'

'That money's to buy myself some guns – the Cheyenne took the others.'

Quinn flushed. 'Now I just might have somethin' to say about that!'

Madigan shrugged. 'Say away. Your local gunsmith

won't sell me a gun, maybe I'll take one of yours.'

Quinn couldn't believe what he was hearing. '*Christ,* man! Are you plumb loco?'

'I'm not leaving town till I find out *exactly* what happened to Red Haskell and why everyone's so leery of talking about him.'

'Hell, *I'm* talkin' about him!'

'But you're not saying anything, Quinn. What you want to do is get me out of town pronto. Feed me what you figure is enough to satisfy my curiosity, then kick me out.'

Quinn frowned, plainly perplexed. After a time he lowered the hammer on his sixgun and holstered the weapon. He took out the makings and rolled a cigarette. He handed the sack and papers to Madigan who rolled a smoke a little awkwardly because his left arm was still in a sling. The sheriff used one match to light both.

'Are you law?' Quinn asked suddenly, and Madigan shook his head.

'I'm a bronc-buster, which is why they call me "Bronco". Been working a place up in Montana, the Bearpaw spread, Custer County. Closest town, I think, was Sky Creek. I never got to see it. Too busy bustin' mustangs for Big Jim Struthers. Heard of him?'

Quinn nodded slowly. 'Scotsman, ain't he? Come out to work his own place, not like a lot of 'em just settin' back in the Highlands waitin' for the Yankee dollars to roll in.'

Madigan nodded. 'Check with Jim. He'll tell you when I left. I'd made some money, figured to take my time getting another job. Was in the wrong place at the wrong time when that Cheyenne war party hit me – and Red Haskell came along and died saving me. You can see why I want to do what I can for his memory.'

Quinn drew on his cigarette, staring hard at Madigan, then nodded slowly. 'I just might send off a couple of wires to Sky Creek.'

That didn't worry Madigan. Jim Struthers was a friend of the US Marshals and would back any story. The lynching and Madigan's failure to get to the bottom of it in Sky Creek would never be mentioned.

'Why you actin' so tough all the time?' Quinn asked after a short silence.

'It's your town that's acting tough. I thought I asked reasonable questions.'

Quinn thought about it. 'You hear about my night deputies, Carnaby and Reed?' Madigan shook his head. 'Worked-over somethin' pitiful. Whoever done it knew what he was about. Must've noticed Carnaby was left-handed and busted his left collarbone, cripplin' his gun arm. Hit him in the throat, too, so he can't hardly speak. Reed got his face all busted and his jaw's wired-up. He can't speak, neither – but he managed to write a coupla things.'

'About who attacked him?' Madigan asked, feigning little interest.

'Yeah. Never seen him properly, but had the impression the man hit him with whatever he used just in one hand.' Quinn looked pointedly at Madigan's left arm in its black sling. 'Doc and Marion Tucker say you were out walkin' round the town about the time they was attacked.'

Madigan snapped his fingers. 'Hell, I heard it! Yelling and groaning – thought it was a fight. Mentioned it to Doc when I got back.'

'And never went to see if you could help out!'

Madigan smiled crookedly. 'Hell, Quinn, I've only got one good arm – what could I do?'

He thought the sheriff was going to draw and shoot him on the spot, but Quinn managed to get himself under control. He dragged deeply and jerkily on his cigarette and tossed it to the ground, mashing it into the stinking earth with his boot.

Then Swede came shuffling back in and offered Madigan fifty dollars, but Quinn snapped at the man to make it a hundred, then told him to go dunk his head in a pail of water three times and pull it out twice. Swede shuffled off, muttering angrily.

'Dumb lunkhead! Look, Madigan, I can run you out of town and I've a mind to, but I've got a pain in the middle of my gut which is what I get when I have a hunch about something – a *bad* hunch. So I'm going to tell you about Red Haskell and why this town don't want to know him. You ready for it?'

Madigan had that bad feeling of his own again and nodded tightly.

Quinn bared his teeth and said,

'The town lynched him the night you brought him back, because he had committed one of the most brutal murders this Territory's ever seen.'

6
'Step Aside!'

Another lynching!

Well, he ought to have read the signs. He had been suspicious of several things on their own, but if he had put them together he would have seen that they could add up to only one thing – a damn lynch party!

First there had been the broken glass on the floor of the infirmary and the split leg of the bedside table – all speaking of rough handling; the replacement bed, carried in by Carnaby and Reed under Marion Tucker's supervision; the wary attitudes of Marion and her husband, the doctor; the hangdog, eye-avoiding towns-folk, except when they did make eye-contact for a moment the looks were afire with hostility; the lack of help for himself; the trampled grave in the pauper's section of the cemetery; the smashing of the half-finished headstone, and the beating of McCann and the stage-line clerk.

Total them up and what did you have?

All classic signs of a town that had gone out of control – willingly enough – but in the cold light of day had to come to terms with the fact that they had hanged another human being without allowing him due process of the law of the land. Guilty without fair trial. Executed by mob rule.

Shame and contrition, hostility to anyone seeking even a remote connection to the man they had lynched. . . .

'You should never've brought Red Haskell back to this town.'

Quinn's hard-edged voice cut through Madigan's thoughts and he snapped his head around, the look in his eyes bringing a frown to the sheriff's face.

'I didn't – I let his horse have its head, figuring if he was from some nearby ranch it'd find its way back. Instead it came here.'

'Uh-huh, so that's how it was. You say you ain't a lawman, Madigan, but were you ever?'

Madigan's gaze didn't waver. 'Uh-huh,' he said, echoing the sheriff. 'I've turned a dollar or two with my gun backed by a badge.'

'Long ago?' Quinn sounded a little more friendly now, as if pleased with himself that his hunch was not altogether wrong.

'What's it matter?' Madigan's voice was harsh. '*You're* the law here – and you were conveniently out of town when they lynched Red.'

There was cold, broad accusation in his words and manner and he wasn't backing down an inch, unarmed or not.

'You get your facts right before you start hintin' that I knew anythin' about the lynchin' in advance, mister!' The sheriff made a menacing move with his hand towards his gun butt, but Madigan's attitude didn't change.

'Did you?'

Quinn swore. 'You just love meetin' trouble head-on don't you, Madigan?'

'*Did* you?' Madigan asked again, just as quietly, just as stubbornly.

Jackson Quinn flushed. 'No, I damn well didn't! You want to know, it was a genuine call out of town – a stabbin' out at a ranch. The Broken Rock on Medicine Creek.'

'Bad one?'

Quinn shrugged. 'Coupla fellers fightin' over a half-breed gal. Rancher tossed 'em in the root cellar and sent for me.'

'And what'd you do about it?'

'By God, Madigan, I don't like your tone!'

The marshal simply waited, as expressionless as a statue – and as unmoving.

'I kicked their butts off the ranch and told 'em to clear the county. Now that's all I'm sayin'. What I do ain't no business of yours.'

'If it had anything to do with making Red Haskell's lynching easier it does.' He held up a hand as Quinn's face darkened. 'Tell me about the murder he was s'posed to've done.'

'Not "s'posed" to've – he done it all right. But if you want to know, let's go back to my office.'

Madigan had no argument with that and in the musty law office, Quinn brought out a bottle of cheap whiskey and held it out towards Madigan, arching his eyebrows in query. Madigan shrugged and Quinn poured a couple of shots into smeared glasses. The sheriff tossed his down but Madigan only sipped, the liquor burning his lips, tongue and throat.

'That how a man drinks his likker where you come from?' Quinn asked with a sneer, topping-up his own glass.

'It's how I drink when I don't really feel like drinking,' Madigan said flatly. 'Tell me about Red Haskell.'

Quinn sighed, leaned back in his chair, ran a hand through his thinning hair. 'Well, sir, Red wasn't a bad young feller. Had a temper to go with that hair and he got into a few scrapes but nothin' too bad. Though he did beat a feller almost to death once ... did six months on our chaingang for it. Seemed to straighten him out.'

'He have family?'

'S'posed to be a sister somewheres, dunno for sure. No, he was just a local cowhand, went from spread to spread, followed the work, did an occasional trail drive into Cheyenne or Laramie.'

'How was he with women?'

Quinn snapped a narrow-eyed look in Madigan's direction. 'You get right down to it, don't you?'

'The way you spoke about that murder made me think it might've been a woman who was killed.'

A strange uncertain and wary look crossed Quinn's rugged features and his hands locked and unlocked a couple of times before he continued.

'Well, guess you saw for yourself that Red was a fairly good-lookin' feller. . . .'

'Didn't really notice, what with the fever and his beard and all the dirt and blood.'

'Take it from me, he was good-lookin' and the gals chased him. Naturally, he took advantage of it, but there was this one gal, Mandy Evans, a real looker, had the fellers in three counties with their tongues hangin' out. But she din' seem interested in any of the fellers around here. Includin' Red. Was talk she'd go into Cheyenne from time to time and join up with the local society there – balls and dinners and such. Guess she felt she was a mite too good for Nightowl Crick.'

'Why'd she stay?'

Quinn shrugged. 'No idea. She kept a dressmakin' shop and that let her travel a bit, down to Denver and Kansas City and so on. Employed local folk. Well, what I'm sayin' is Red Haskell was smitten with her. Besotted – the one gal he couldn't have, see, so he wanted her most of all.'

Madigan frowned a little but said nothing.

'He tried and tried and seems Mandy might've led him on at one stage, just a little – only she'd know why. But he tied one on after a big round-up that put a big bonus in his pocket and he bought her flowers and chocolates and all that kinda stuff, got himself spruced-up and went a'callin'. . . .' He paused and sighed, shaking his head. 'She laughed at him. Now I know this don't make Mandy seem all that fine a woman but she was a mite different class to the kind we get in these sort of towns. I don't think she meant anythin' by it other than that his efforts amused her—'

'But to Red it was a straight insult,' cut in Madigan. 'To most men it would be.'

'Yea-aah – that was it. He got drunker'n a skunk and went back, kicked her door down and – guess he tried to force himself on her. Place was all smashed up when we found her. She'd been beaten and kicked to death, cut up somethin' awful. Man, all that beautiful flesh all torn and mangled. . . . Doc couldn't even be sure if she'd been raped, but if she had been it was after she'd been killed. An' this is the man you want a headstone for!'

Madigan's jaw knotted. 'He still saved my life. *That's* what the marker's for. How come Red got the blame?'

Quinn spread his hands. 'Hell, man, a bunch of folk saw and heard him kick Mandy's door in.'

'And no one tried to stop him?'

'Hey, Red was mighty handy with his fists – and a gun, too. No one figured he'd do much, though, way he was staggerin' they thought he'd be too damn drunk to even climb the stairs.'

'And who saw him kill the girl?'

The sheriff blinked. 'No one *saw* him, for Chris'sakes!'

'Then how d'you know he did it? Maybe he found her already dead. Maybe they argued and he left if he was as drunk as your witnesses say, couldn't hope to do anything with the gal so just left. Anyone could've gone in after him if the door was already busted.'

Quinn stood slowly, leaning his hands on his desk

edge. 'You sure you're not still a lawman?' Madigan said nothing but Quinn didn't look any more relaxed. He took a turn around the small office. 'I seen enough to figure Red done it. His knife was there with his initials carved in the staghorn handle. It'd been used to mutilate the gal, accordin' to Doc Tucker, size and shape of the blade fitted the cuts. Witnesses seen him go in. Everyone knew he wanted to bed Mandy – and she'd been stupid enough to laugh in his face when he tried to do things the way he figured she'd like. It had to be him.'

'You went to trial with that evidence?'

Quinn came back to his chair and sat down slowly. He leaned on his elbows, hands locked on the desk before him. He shook his head.

'No trial. Red broke outa jail – and I still think he had help – and ran for the hills. We had posses out for days but no one knew them hills better'n Red. He'd worked for every ranch in the county and beyond, knew every bush and hidey-hole. We lost him and only thing I could think of was to wait him out. Figured he'd get tired of bein' without a woman and show up somewhere we could get a line on him, but you very nicely brung him back and dumped him in our laps.'

Madigan stood slowly. 'Not for you to lynch.'

'Hey! *I* had nothin' to do with the lynchin'! You were closer to it than me! They drug him outa the infirmary only a few feet away from you.'

Madigan nodded, mouth grim. 'That's something I'll have to live with – I never heard a thing. No, wait! Thought I was having nightmares from the fever.

Recollect a lot of voices, some shouting, glass smashing. There'd been talk of a lynching in Sky Creek in Montana before I got here. Thought it must've been in my mind. . . .' He slowed his speech and nodded slowly. 'I was dog-sick next morning. I know that feeling now: too much chloroform, I've had operations before. I figure Doc Tucker must've given me an overdose so I wouldn't wake up early and see the lynch party.'

'Now wait a minute!' Quinn hurried around his desk and stood between Madigan and the door. 'You can't go around accusin' a man like Doc Tucker of that kinda thing!'

'Step aside, Quinn,' Madigan said quietly. 'You're gonna be surprised at what I can and can't do. This lynching stinks and so does that murder. But in any case, whether Red killed that girl or not, I still owe him my life and I aim to find out for *sure* just what really did happen to Mandy Evans.'

Quinn's Colt palmed up smoothly, menaced Madigan. 'No you don't! This is my town, mister, and you're no one but a drifter so you obey me! I'm the law here! You start steppin' on toes in this town and we'll find you a place right alongside Red up on Boot Hill!'

Madigan smiled thinly. 'Thanks, Quinn, you just made it that much easier. . . .'

'What?' The sheriff was plainly puzzled.

'You just told me the town does have something to hide. Now nothing'll stop me. Not even your gun.'

On the last word, Madigan's right hand moved like a striking snake, thumb and finger pinching the fluted cylinder so that even if Quinn strained his utmost at the trigger it couldn't possibly turn, which meant the weapon couldn't fire. Then he stomped on Quinn's left instep and the man sucked in a sharp breath and stumbled. When he straightened, Madigan had the sixgun in his hand.

He smiled at the angry sheriff, stepped to the door that led to the cell block and skidded the gun right along the passage. He shouldered the limping lawman aside and went out into the street.

There was a slight noise behind him and, as he started to turn, Quinn's voice bellowed, '*Madigan!*'

The marshal came round quickly, ready to dive to one side and froze when he saw that the sheriff held a twin-barrelled shotgun in his hands. Even as he watched, Quinn cocked both hammers.

'I'm the law here, Madigan! You remember that! Any investigatin' to be done, I'll do it! Now that's all I got to say on the matter except – if you're stubborn enough, *stupid* enough, to butt into what don't concern you, well, you only got yourself to blame for whatever happens.'

'You got a nice turn of phrase, Quinn. I understood every word you said.'

'Then savvy this, too: the stage leaves at four this afternoon.'

'Thanks for the info. Anyone asks me I'll be able to tell 'em.'

'Madigan! You be on it!'

Madigan smiled and threw the man a half-salute,

turned and walked across the street towards the gunsmith's.

'*You be on it! Hear?*'

7

Armed and Dangerous

The gunsmith was surly but he didn't make much fuss about selling Madigan a Colt and a full-length Winchester rifle with a flip-up peep-sight, leather scabbard, holster, boxes of ammunition and some gunsmithing tools.

'You here for the lynching?' Madigan asked casually.

The gunsmith turned slowly, a rail-lean man with long hair and hooked nose. His eyes settled on the marshal's face. 'Know nothin' about any lynchin'.'

'It happened, friend,' Madigan said tautly.

'Then guess I must've slept right through it,' the man said flatly. 'Ain't the kinda thing that'd interest me. I'm a family man.'

'So're most of the men in town but that didn't stop 'em stringing up a man they had no real idea was guilty or not.'

The gunsmith sighed, looking tough.

'That's them – not me. If you're lookin' to try out the guns, there's a small draw just past the west end of town, 'bout half-a-mile after you cross the bridge over the crick.'

Madigan nodded, picked up his parcels and left. That was likely about as much help as he could expect to get from the rest of the town, too, he figured.

He spent a long time shooting-in the guns, especially the Colt. It was new and stiff and rough. He took it apart expertly, worked on it with fine screwdrivers and pointed-nose pliers and a file. By the time he had finished he had halved the trigger-pull, smoothed-out the sear and adjusted the hammer spring so that it came back easily under his thumb. He fired single shots with deliberate aim, emptied the cylinder with fast trigger-work, fired by slipping the hammer, using his thumb only with the trigger fully depressed.

He hadn't lost his touch, though he figured he was maybe a hair slower on the draw. But some neat's-foot oil rubbed and worked into the holster tonight would overcome that.

He needed both hands for shooting the rifle, a heavy, octagonal barrel beyond the wood fore-end needing to be balanced or supported. He took his injured arm out of the sling, worked the shoulder, kneaded the muscles around the stitched gash, flexed stiff fingers. It would do for now but to make sure he didn't strain it, he cut a small forked stick and rested the rifle's barrel in this while he picked out his targets at the far end of the draw, about 200 yards distant.

The Winchester shot high and to the right. He used

the pliers on the buckhorn rear sight, gave the foresight a slight tweak and did this a few times until he was hitting where he aimed. He set the peepsight then and was able to blow stones the size of a walnut to dust way down at the far end of the draw.

He used two boxes of cartridges and had just emptied the rifle when there was a violent puff of dust in front of his face and he reared back, eyes stinging from spurting gravel.

He was belly-down on a slope and slid back down, hearing the echoing flat crack of the rifle as it tried for him twice more. The bullets were close and he knew he was dealing with a marksman – and a cautious one at that. The man had waited until the rifle was empty before he had tried his first, ranging shot. And Madigan glimpsed the gunsmoke up on the rim and saw that the rifleman had also made sure he was out of effective range of the sixgun which was fully loaded and in Madigan's new holster buckled round his waist with the belt's bullet-loops filled to capacity.

He hit the bottom running and dived behind a rock as a fourth bullet ricocheted, ploughing sandstone just above his head. Panting, Madigan twisted onto his back, grunting at the pain as his gashed shoulder hit a rock. He thought he felt a little trickle of blood but that was the least of his worries at the moment, as he fumbled shells out of the belt loops and thumbed them through the rifle's loading-gate.

With five thrust home, he spun onto his belly, lunged right and hit rolling, hurting his shoulder again as he scrabbled in behind another sandstone rock. He flung himself at the rock, elbow jamming against the gritty, sloping surface, cupped hand supporting the rifle's fore-end as he drew on the rimrock through the peepsight. The man up there was moving, looking for him.

Madigan's shot kicked dust from the man's grey shirt sleeve, sent him stumbling out of sight, his startled curse barely reaching Madigan's ears. He placed two more shots on the edge of the rimrock and stones flew, humming.

There was no answering shot.

Madigan took his chance, leaped up and started running for the entrance to the draw, figuring the rifleman was making a dash for it now that Madigan had located him and reloaded.

He was too late. The man had had a horse waiting and by the time Madigan cleared the draw and topped the small rise between it and the bridge over the creek, the man was riding over that bridge, hoofs thudding in a brief hollow tattoo, as he skidded into the stand of timber, getting more cover between him and Madigan so that he could race directly for town.

Madigan stood there, panting, sweating a little, fully loaded the rifle's magazine this time, went back to his position and refilled the empty loops in his belt, then gathered his things and started back to town.

He used the back streets, waded the creek and entered the gunsmith's quietly through the rear door.

The man was just buttoning the fresh shirt he had put on in a small cubicle behind the counter. The front door had a *Closed* sign dangling in the glass panel. The gunsmith almost put his head through the low ceiling when Madigan stepped into the doorway of the cubicle. There was a rough bandage on the man's left arm. 'Get the hell outa here!'

Madigan said nothing, used the rifle barrel to lift the grey shirt with the bullet-torn sleeve off the floor. The gunsmith swallowed, started to bluster again, but Madigan flung the shirt across his face, muffling him. As the man clawed at the sweaty shirt, Madigan reversed the rifle and drove the butt brutally into the gunsmith's skinny midriff. He gagged and dropped to his knees. The shirt fell away from his contorted face and there was fear in his eyes now. Madigan drove the brass butt-plate against the man's forehead, splitting the skin, knocking him sprawling into a corner. Then he stomped on the man's right hand with his riding boot, turned and walked out, patting the sweated, dust-caked horse that had its rein ends looped loosely over a hitching post in the back yard.

The shoulder wound was busted open and bleeding again and Doc Tucker seemed nervous as he sewed it up once more, Marion crouching beside Madigan's chair, holding the bowl of blood-tinged antiseptic.

'You need to take more care, Mr Madigan,' admonished Tucker.

'You're right there, Doc. Someone tried to kill me earlier.' Man and wife exchanged a swift look, Marion sucking in a sharp breath. Madigan told them briefly what had happened, although he said nothing about trailing the gunsmith to his store. 'So, like you say, Doc, I need to be more careful.'

'Well, this will leave a nasty, twisted scar, which I doubt will worry you much, but it's prone to reinfection easily, so—'

'Long as you don't have to give me any chloroform to repair it, Doc,' Madigan said, looking the man straight in the eye and seeing Tucker flush. Marion almost dropped the bowl.

'I – er – had no choice the other night.'

'Sure you did, Doc, you had a choice.' Madigan's voice was hard and his face was unrelenting. 'The whole town had a choice. They simply chose lynching instead of a fair trial for a man they'd decided was already guilty.'

'Look, Mr Madigan, you're a stranger here and you don't fully understand—' began Marion, but the look on his face stopped her.

'I savvy that I was KO'd with chloroform so that I either couldn't witness or interfere with the mob who came in to drag out a man who had just had his gut sliced open by an arrow and one leg amputated. Wouldn't you think, Doc, that even a goddamn drunken lynch mob would have grabbed him *before* you put him through that amputation!'

Marion made a small cry, set down the bowl and hurried from the room, a hand over her lower face. Tucker tied off thread with trembling fingers and cleared his throat. There was a trace of anger in his next words.

'You never saw that poor girl, how she was muti-lated!'

'Doc, you're as bad as the men who led that lynch

party and I'm serving notice on you that I'm gonna see every one of the sons of bitches pay for what they did.'

'Good Lord, man! Who d'you think you are, coming in here and deciding what's right and what's wrong? What gives you the right. . . ?'

'You know the answer to that, Doc.' Madigan stood after Tucker covered the newly stitched wound with gauze and adhesive tape and rolled down his sleeve.

'Red Haskell may've saved your life, but he was a cold-blooded murderer! As I said, you didn't *see* that poor girl like I did. I had to do an autopsy on her. Animals don't treat their own kind as barbarically as Mandy Evans was treated.'

'Whoever did it has to pay, Doc, I admit, but I'm not certain sure it was Red Haskell. Even if it *was*, he was still entitled to a trial.'

'He lost all entitlements to be treated as a human being! He deserved to die the way he did.'

Madigan's eyes narrowed. 'Doc, I'm beginning to think you did that amputation first just to make him suffer.'

Tucker went white, unable to reply.

'If I find out that's so, I'll burn this infirmary down around you, Doc – and the rest of this lousy town, too. You can count on that.'

He stopped at the beds of Carnaby and Reed on the way out.

'How're you doing, gents? Think they'll ever get the feller who beat you up?' There were unintelligible growls from both and Madigan smiled coldly. 'I reckon they've got about as much chance as they have of finding the mangy coyotes who crippled McCann and that stage-line clerk, you ask me . . . sleep well, gents.'

No one would rent Madigan a room in town so he went out to the northern edge where there were several abandoned stores and cabins. Every one of them needed some work but Madigan managed to fix up one near the creek, which gave him ready access to water and deadfalls supplied him with firewood. He used the butt of his Colt for a hammer, pulled rusty nails out of old boards and straightened them with the pliers. By sundown he had a liveable place, although he had to bring in green boughs from along the creek for a bed.

He caught a fish in the creek, built a small fire and roasted it in the coals. Then he went back up to the town, noticing that there was dim, flickering light, like that cast by a sputtering candle, coming from another of the abandoned cabins several along from the one he had chosen.

He took his rifle with him and made his way to the law office where Jackson Quinn was just finishing his supper, eating off a tray that Madigan figured would have come from the diner a few doors along.

'Was just gonna come lookin' for you,' Quinn said without preamble, sounding annoyed. 'You were s'posed to be on that stage. Instead you been steam-rollerin' through my town – beat-up on Kettle, the gunsmith, and made threats to good ol' Doc Tucker—'

'Uh-huh,' Madigan said coolly and lifted the shiny new rifle, letting the muzzle casually wander in the lawman's direction.

Quinn froze with his coffee mug halfway to his mouth. 'By Christ! Don't you threaten *me!*'

'Who's threatening who, Quinn? Kettle tried to kill me this afternoon.'

'Hogwash! At worst he was only tryin' to throw a scare into you.'

'But you're threatening to throw *me* into jail. You have witnesses to back up your complaints. . . ? Thought not. So it's my word agin Kettle's and the doc's.'

'I dunno about Kettle, but a man like Doc Tucker don't lie – and Marion was likely there.' Madigan shook his head slowly, not speaking, and Quinn swore. 'You're just one big smart-ass, ain't you? No witnesses – which still don't mean I can't throw you in jail while I investigate further.'

Madigan shrugged. 'You want to try, that's your business.'

'Madigan, you're a mighty dangerous man, I figure, and I wouldn't be loco enough to come straight out and call you a liar, but the way you been actin' – well, I ain't sure you're not *still* a lawman! And if you are, you owe it to me to come out in the open so's we can come to some arrangement.'

The marshal laughed briefly. 'I've really got you buffaloed, haven't I, Quinn? Relax. I ain't about to blow your head off if you want to call me a liar – because it don't matter a good goddamn to me what you or anyone else in this dump thinks of me. I told you what I aim to do and I'll do it. All I want from you tonight are my saddle-bags and my warbag if you have it.'

Quinn lowered his coffee cup at last, eased back in his chair, hard eyes not wavering an inch. He studied Madigan in silence for a long minute.

'OK, I've got 'em. And you can have 'em. But next time we lock horns, Madigan, one of us is gonna have trouble walkin' away.' He stood up and said heavily, 'For the last time – *this is my town!* You have any trouble with that, go see Judge Hannibal. He'll tell you I been duly elected, not just some fast gun hired-on to police the town. I know these folk and they look to me for protection, and by God they'll get it. You need to savvy that, and *remember* it!'

'OK, I will. Now where're my things?'

Walking back towards his ramshackle cabin, Madigan kept an eye out for trouble, but his mind was mainly on one thing: this town had a judge he hadn't even known about. Now just what the hell was this Judge Hannibal about allowing a lynch mob to take over? *Maybe he was out of town, too. . . .*

But Quinn was being cagey, maybe *too* damn cagey. He had expected a lot more trouble from the man than he'd had so far. He sure seemed scared that Madigan was some kind of law: he'd likely throw a fit if he knew he was a federal marshal.

Madigan stopped abruptly as he made his way along the creek bank. There was someone in his cabin. He had fixed the door so that it would close but there was no lock on it. He saw now that it stood open and he thumbed back the hammer on his rifle, a cartridge already in the breech.

He set down his warbag and saddle-bags carefully,

moved in a crouch to the doorway, listened to the small sounds inside, then he stepped in, rifle at the ready.

'What the hell're you doing here?'

There was a gasp and a vague shape spun towards him, made a dash for the door, trying to dodge around him. He thrust out a leg and the intruder gave a small cry, sprawling half in and half out of the cabin.

He stepped forward and thrust the rifle barrel towards the panting form.

'Don't shoot! I-I'm just looking for food. I'm – hungry!'

Madigan blinked.

It was the voice of a young woman.

8

Town Backed Up

He had candle stubs in his saddle-bags and used two of these to light the cabin, though there were plenty of shadows – and quite a few rustlings in there, too. The girl looked only slightly perturbed.

She was in her twenties, he figured, with dark hair and kind of brown-green eyes that watched his every move, warily, but not with a great deal of fear. He liked her face, it showed strength, maybe a little eroded by some recent happenings, which gave her a slight edgy look. But he could see she was a fighter and she was dressed in dirt-smeared denim trousers, dusty but good riding boots and a shirt that had been patched in two places. Her figure looked good, what he could see of it in the dim light as she crouched back in one corner.

She told him her name was Catrina Harmon.

'And how come you were trying to steal from me, Catrina?' He gestured around the humble room. 'You can see I don't have much.'

She pushed some of her abundant black hair back off her face. 'I didn't know what you had. I saw you move in this afternoon. I'm hungry, damn hungry! And I have no money. I live in one of those broken-down cabins across there. . . .'

She gestured vaguely in the direction of the place where he had seen the candlelight earlier.

'How come?'

She sighed, settled down, raising her knees and placing her arms across them. 'You're Madigan, aren't you? The man who has this town scared white.'

He smiled slightly, rolled a cigarette silently.

'I was a – friend of Red Haskell's.' That made him straighten. 'They claim I helped him escape from jail.'

'So you're the one. Did you help him?'

She hesitated, just a little too long, so that the hesitation itself was answer enough.

'Red was hot-tempered and he had a real fixation on Mandy Evans, but he wasn't a brutal man or a cruel one. He was wild and sometimes he acted like a spoiled brat, but I know he couldn't have done those terrible things to Mandy.'

She drew a deep breath. 'Just in case you think I'm trying to make out he was some sort of angel, I've also seen him beat a man flat and keep on hitting him even after he had won. . . .'

'So he *could* have killed Mandy Evans, if his temper got out of control?'

'No! I told you he was infatuated with her. Even drunk he wouldn't have done what they say he did. . . .' She paused, looked a little uncertain, then said, 'He admitted he hit her and she fell and hit her head. But she was only knocked out and he was appalled at having hit a woman so he ran.'

'What was his theory? Someone else found her and killed her?'

'Yes! Don't you see, it had to be that way! Red *couldn't* have done those terrible things. He couldn't have!'

Madigan fired-up his cigarette, drew on it and watched her through the smoke he exhaled. 'You were in love with him.'

She flushed. 'I thought I was. But a lot of women thought that about Red. He had a way of making you feel like someone special. He was a rogue at worst where women were concerned, and he got into a lot of fights and someone once claimed he shot a man in Cheyenne. I don't know if it's true, but I've never heard of him mistreating any woman.'

'So you convinced yourself he was innocent and helped him get out of jail.'

Her eyes flashed. 'What else could I do? There was already talk of lynching in the saloons.'

'So you risked your own neck for Red.'

'I told you why. They couldn't be sure I had helped him escape but they were pretty certain, so I've been banished. Suddenly my room was required for an important cattle buyer – who never turned up. I couldn't find accommodation anywhere else in town. Can you believe every room was taken in a dump like this? The livery wouldn't even hire me a horse. I lost my job. . . . Of course, there was never any seat for me on the stage out so I was effectively held a prisoner here.

No one speaks to me. I've used up all my money – they didn't mind taking *that*, although I'm always given inferior goods and served last. I had no choice but to come and live out here. Unless I wanted to walk thirty miles to the nearest ranch.'

'Did you try?'

She nodded. 'Reed and Carnaby brought me back. Jackson Quinn said I'm a suspect in the jailbreak and so I have to stay where he can find me. They watch me night and day. That used to be Carnaby or Reed, too, but now they're out of it – thanks to you. There'll be someone else, though.'

'Never took to this town right from the start. You want to leave? I'll take you out if you do.'

Her eyes roved his gaunt, rugged face, the flickering light and shadows highlighting the hard years and the kind of life he had led.

'I'm sure you would, but I haven't anywhere to go really. . . . But why would you help me?'

'If you know about me, you know Red saved my life – and they lynched him. I can't accept that.'

'You'll be taking on the whole town!'

'Seems I have to.'

'One man against all of Nightowl Creek!'

'Not all of it – you're not against me, are you?'

She laughed briefly, shaking her head slowly. 'Well, you are really something out of the box, Madigan!' She sobered. 'But if you're really going to try to prove Red was or was not guilty, I think I'll stay. You just might need a hand.'

*

Getting food was no problem. He had a little money left and although the storekeeper didn't want to serve him, in the end he bought eggs and bacon and beans and flour and coffee.

The girl cooked them a meal and ate ravenously.

'We better catch some fish or we'll be out of grub in a day or so.'

She smiled. 'Sorry! It's the best food I've had for days.'

She told him there had been three attempts by drunks to break into her cabin. Two of them would not be interested in women for a long time, she said casually. The third had had his face ruined by the splintered end of a branch she was collecting for firewood and would have one hell of a time explaining to his wife just how he had come by the injury.

Madigan grinned. 'I better get you a derringer or something just the same.'

She shrugged. 'If you like. Just what are you going to do, anyway?'

'Go see this Judge Hannibal first. Don't like the sound of any judge who'd stand by and let a lynch party have their way and do nothing about it afterwards.'

'Ye-es. He doesn't get around much. He's a sick man, maybe dying, I don't know. Sheriff Quinn seems to have most of the say if there's any real trouble. Gives a man a few weeks on the chain gang or a few days in his cells – I think he has Judge Hannibal's blessing – if that's the right word.'

'No, it's not. It smells of laziness and maybe corruption.'

She looked at him strangely. 'They say you could be a lawman. . . .'

'So they say – reckon I'll just keep 'em guessing.'

'Me, too?'

He nodded curtly and she flushed slightly. 'Where's the judge's house?'

'He won't appreciate you going to his house at this time of night.'

'Won't bother me. How do I find it?'

She gave him directions and he left the rifle with her. She said she would wait for him right here in his cabin.

The house overlooked the deep bend of the creek where willows and lush grass would be easy on the eye. The place was two-storeyed, clapboard, the paint in good condition. A tough-looking servant refused Madigan entry but he pushed by anyway and strode into a parlour.

Judge Hannibal was sitting reading, wearing a robe tied around his skinny middle. He looked sallow and sick, gaunt face sagging and lined. His grey hair stood out in tufts and he sat up with a jerk when Madigan entered.

The servant appeared behind Madigan, hard-eyed, his hands fisted-up. 'Sorry, Judge – will I throw him out?'

Hannibal held up a bony hand, the flesh thin and almost transparent, never taking his eyes off Madigan. 'Leave us, Leon,' he said in a mellow voice, and the man hesitated briefly before going out and closing the door after him. The judge looked soberly at his caller. 'And to what do I owe the pleasure of your visit, Mr Madigan?'

'Not much pleasure intended, Judge. Just want to know how come you sat still for a lynching.'

'Had no choice, man! I don't get around very well. I heard the racket, of course, but it was all over before Leon had my wheelchair readied for me. Anyway, Red Haskell's no loss.'

'Maybe not to you.'

'Oh, I know all about him saving your life, Mr Madigan, very heroic of him. I understand your concern, but the fact remains the man was a murderer.'

'And didn't get a chance of having a fair trial.'

The judge spread his thin hands. 'This is a frontier town, Mr Madigan. Surely you've been around long enough to know that passions can get out of hand quickly when some lovely young woman like Mandy Evans is brutalized and murdered! Good God, I wouldn't have hesitated to haul on the rope myself if I'd had the strength.'

'Which just goes to show you ain't doing your job here, Judge. You're not fit to be in a position where you have the right of life and death over anyone.'

Hannibal's rheumy eyes narrowed. 'That's not for you to say. And I think I've had enough of this – interview. You may leave now.'

'Judge, I'll be glad to lose your company as quickly as possible, but I want you to savvy something before I go – I'll be back for you. And anyone else who figures they can get away with a lynching. I'll wipe out the whole damn town if I have to.'

He wouldn't have thought it possible for Hannibal to get any paler but his face took on a death-like pallor and the thin hands grasped at the arms of his chair.

'*Get out!* I will not have anyone speaking to me in that manner in my own house. *Get out, I say!*'

Madigan paused as he started for the door. 'Remember, Judge, I'll be back. . . .'

'This way,' growled Leon from the doorway, a hand near a gun he now wore on his hip.

Madigan winked as he stepped past. 'See you later.'

He left as Leon scowled and Jackson Quinn entered the judge's parlour by a second door.

'He's a hardcase, that Madigan, ain't he?'

'He . . . he's a most dangerous man. He can – and will – cause us a lot of trouble, Jackson. I think it best that he be taken care of – very quickly.'

'I'm still worried that he's some kinda lawman, Judge,' the sheriff said, really looking worried, too.

Hannibal nodded gently, his breathing gradually settling back to normal. 'Yes, he has the look – and the manner. But he's very, very tough, Jackson. He *must* be taken care of! Can't you fix it so that it appears to be personal?'

Quinn thought for a short time, then nodded, smiling crookedly. 'Believe I have just the men, Judge. Now you rest easy: Madigan won't give us no more trouble – whoever he is. Guarantee it!'

The girl wasn't at Madigan's cabin when he returned and there was no light burning in her own shack. Hand on gun butt, he went looking for her and she stepped out of the shadows near her own cabin, holding his rifle.

'I'm here,' she said a little breathlessly. 'I waited outside in case someone tried to trap me in the cabin.'

'Good thinking.'

She didn't invite him in but led the way back towards his cabin. He went in with his sixgun in his hand, but it was safe and he lit the candle stub and told her about his brief visit with Judge Hannibal.

'That feller Leon seems to be his bodyguard.'

She looked at him steadily and shook her head wonderingly. 'You sure do like to provoke your enemies!'

'That's the way I work. Stir 'em up, get 'em guessing, get 'em edgy. That's when folk start making mistakes.'

'And you pounce . . . you *are* a lawman, aren't you?'

'Quinn mentioned once that he thought Red Haskell had a sister somewhere,' he said, deliberately ignoring her question. 'You ever hear about her?'

Her brown-green eyes were slightly narrowed as she pursed her lips slowly. 'Yes, he mentioned a married sister. Husband killed in a riding accident a few years back – not far from here. A place called – let me see – Forked Lightning? No-oo . . . not quite. Pitchfork? Something with "fork" in the brand anyway. . . .'

'You know where?'

She shook her head. 'Not exactly. I'm a town girl, hardly ever stick my nose outside of Nightowl Creek. But Red used to see her once in a while. Somewhere out towards Medicine Creek, near a spur of the range he called Bowleg. North-west, I think. I know her married name is Morton – Peggy I think he called her. He didn't speak about her much. Are you going to see her?'

'Reckon so – if they'll hire me a horse.'

She left for her own shack soon after, refusing his offer of the rifle or sixgun, saying with confidence that she wouldn't be bothered, but if she was, she could take care of herself.

Next morning, the Swede refused to hire a mount to Madigan.

'You already gypped me outa a hunnered bucks. I don't do you no more favours . . . an' you ain't got the sher'ff to back you up this time.'

'No,' admitted Madigan easily. 'So I'll just have to take what I want myself.'

'Now, listen, you!' The Swede reached for a sawn-off shotgun on his bench and Madigan's sixgun whispered out of leather, the barrel cracking across the man's thick wrist. He hugged his injured hand against his body as Madigan took the shotgun.

'Swede, I got no time to play about. Get me a good hoss and saddle. You can tell me how much I owe you when I get back.'

'I not give you horse!'

Madigan sighed, swung the shotgun's barrels hard into the man's midriff and, when he doubled-up, clubbed him to the ground.

The Swede was still out to it when Madigan rode a wide-stepping grey through the doors twenty minutes later. He took the shotgun with him and stopped at Catrina's shack, offering it to her.

'Belongs to Swede, but you keep it handy till I get back – just in case.'

'You be careful, Madigan! It can be a dangerous trail out there.'

'Used to them.'

He stopped at the Wells Fargo Agency before leaving town. His money had been wired through, $200.

It ought to be enough, he figured. He left fifty dollars with Mel McConnell who lived behind the stage depot and whose wife took the money – *snatched* the money from him and told him he was a tightwad.

'Man beat half to death and it's worth only fifty dollars!' she almost spat at him.

He sighed, gave her another twenty, feeling bad that he couldn't spare more.

Then he started out of town towards the north-western trail, under the hostile eyes of the townsfolk.

He knew every last one of them was hoping he was leaving for good.

9
Danger Trail

It seemed to be a well-travelled trail, leading out through boulder-strewn country with dips and hollows and several dry watercourses. There was scattered timber, too, clumps and big stretches of brush, the land lifting towards the Bowleg Spur of the Medicine Bows.

Mighty good ambush country.

So Bronco Madigan rode carefully, rifle across his thighs, eyes alert, but the birds that wheeled and dived and chattered seemed content and unalarmed and he began to relax. It was hot, the heat beating at him like a hammer from the rounded, lichen-scabbed faces of the boulder fields. Catrina had told him of a waterhole just past the halfway mark, down between two ridges, in the shadow of a red-rock wall.

'I think it's an old Indian well,' she had said. 'I've never been there but Red mentioned it once or twice.'

It might well be a source of water used by Indians, but not necessarily an "old" one and all that that implied – abandoned, avoided for some reason.

So he went in warily, found the shadowed water like a black hole in the earth, a mirror undisturbed by the faint hot breeze that wafted through the boulder fields. Once again, birds were drinking at the edges and flew off casually when he dismounted and led the grey in.

The horse drank and he pulled it away before it could bloat, ground-hitched it some distance away while he went back with his canteen. He filled this first, and set down his rifle, taking one last cautious look around before he stretched out and plunged his hot, dusty face into the cool liquid.

He swallowed one mouthful and then the surface beside his head was torn by a bullet and, as he rolled back and away, snatching at his rifle, he heard the report of the shot, slapping around the ridges.

It was followed by a volley that told him at least two rifles were seeking him as he continued to roll down the slope up against the wall. The bullet placement had driven him in here and he knew that he had fallen into the trap laid by the killers.

There was a slight inward angle to the red rock wall, not enough to be called an overhang, just enough to send bullets skidding down to where he lay.

Grit and coarse sand kicked into his face and he got his boots against the rock and snapped his legs straight, launching himself like an arrow – into the pool itself.

He already knew it was deep and he plunged under, clawing at the bottom, fingers skidding off the slippery rocks. Above him, bullets *zipped* and *thrupped* as the killers raked the surface. Instead of coming up on the side where he had been drinking, he lunged left and heaved out of the shallows in one muscle-wrenching leap. This was the side nearest the slope away from the wall and he spun over and over, grit and grass clinging to his sodden clothes. He had caught them unawares, but only for a few seconds and then the lead began punching into the earth around his sliding body.

He got his feet beneath him, saw the cover he wanted – a deadfall angled across a corner of the rock wall – and dived for it headlong. He hit hard and the breath slammed out of him as he hurt his injured shoulder, but by the time he had landed and scrabbled in close to the log, he had the lever working on the rifle, praying that its newness and remnants of the coating of packing grease would keep the mechanism working. His cartridges should be waterproof enough after such a small immersion.

The big Winchester thudded and he saw rock explode a foot to the left of where he had aimed. Frowning, he adjusted the peepsight but saw that it was angled over to one side. He must have hit it hard when he had dived into the pool. He flipped it down and used the buckhorn and blade sights, placing his next shot closer to the mark.

The twin guns thundered, raked his cover, splinters exploding, rock chips falling on his shoulder as he hunched down under the log. Then he was up on one knee and the rifle hammered and he glimpsed something white up there that gave a sudden jerk and disappeared from sight. There was a brief silence, the echoes of the shots dying slowly. Then a gun spoke once more, but from several yards to the left. He swung his blade foresight in that direction, centred it in the buckhorn and took a steadying breath, waiting. A hat appeared first, then a blocky outline of a head and one shoulder and a rifle. Madigan partly released his breath, steadied, set his aim and caressed the trigger. Thanks to his work on the firing mechanism, it let off smoothly without the slightest jerk. The butt punched at his shoulder and he glimpsed the hat sailing above the ridge up there, thought he heard a kind of strangled yelp.

He held his fire but the man didn't shoot again from that position. In fact he didn't shoot again at all. The silence dragged on and then he heard the clatter of hoofs and he was up and leaping over his deadfall, running for the grey. He hit saddle with a grunt and the horse protested briefly, but then he had it running across the slope towards the lowest part of the ridge, rifle held out to one side for balance. The grey got into its stride and seemed to enjoy itself as it bunched its powerful muscles and took him up and over the ridge.

He was ready for gunfire but none came – at first. As he was thundering down the far side a rifle cracked behind and slightly above. The bullet was wide and he hipped in time to see a man half-lying behind a rock, trying to get under cover better, one arm heavily bandaged. The man seemed to be wounded and slumped as if unconscious so Madigan held his fire, turned back to the chase.

He spotted the fleeing bushwhacker, hatless now, lashing his mount into some boulders. Madigan stood in the stirrups, found balance easily as he let the grey have its head, beaded the man, led him by a yard, and squeezed off his shot. The killer's horse went down as if pole-axed, throwing its rider heavily. The man somersaulted and skidded, dust rising, the horse tumbling down and over him. But he got out without catching a hoof in the face or head apparently, for in moments he was stumbling to his feet, dragging at his sixgun as he turned to face the oncoming Madigan.

Madigan recognized him as he rode the man down, the grey's impact hurling him several feet. As Madigan dismounted, the killer rose to his knees, palming up his sixgun, panting, face streaked with blood.

Madigan drew and fired instinctively and the man was slammed back, hitting on his shoulders, lower body lifting with the driving force, before crumpling in a heap. Madigan swore, knowing he had killed the man, and walked forward, kneeling and feeling for the big vein in the grimy neck to make sure.

He felt the wiring beneath the skin of the jaw and knew why the man had made such a strangled sound when the bullet had wrenched the hat from his head. This was Billy-Jack Reed, apparently having left his sick bed for the chance to bushwhack Madigan. And the other one, with the heavily bandaged, or plastered, arm had to be Sel Carnaby.

Madigan swung into the saddle and rode back to where the wounded Carnaby had been lying in the rocks. The man strained to lift his rifle one-handed, his face almost as white as the plaster cast on his left arm. Madigan leaned almost casually from the saddle and slammed the gun from his hands with his heavy rifle barrel. He dismounted and stood over the downed man. Carnaby glared his hatred and he cursed in a strangled voice, his neck still bruised from where Madigan had hit him with the pick handle.

As Madigan sat down on a rock within a couple of feet, Carnaby made one desperate heave to the side and brought up his sixgun from under his leg. It roared and Madigan tumbled off his rock, his own Colt thundering across his body. Carnaby was smashed back by the bullet taking him in the chest and Madigan knelt beside him, tossing the man's gun out of reach.

'You're game, Carnaby, but a goddamn fool – I act instinctively when someone tries to shoot me. I shoot to kill.'

And Carnaby was dying now and knew it. His previous wound was high on his right thigh and likely wouldn't have caused him much trouble, but the second bullet was mortal and he must have known it, but he still glared bitter hatred at Madigan.

'This your own idea?' the marshal asked. 'Or did Quinn send you?'

Carnaby tried to spit at him, but the bloody froth only trickled down his chin. Madigan sighed, stood, reloading the empty chambers in the Colt's cylinder. 'Damn it, Carnaby, you could've told me a good deal, I reckon . . . but I'll let you have your last minutes in peace.'

Madigan walked away, hearing the man's rasping, bubbling breathing quicken and then drop back to irregular gasps. By the time he was mounted on the grey and had his rifle's magazine reloaded it had stopped.

There was already a buzzard high in the sky, circling above Reed's sprawled body.

An hour later he came to a fork in the trail with some weathered wooden signs on a sagging hickory post. One said *Arrow* and pointed up the left fork. The other said *Wildfire* and there was a crude bolt of forked lightning burned into the board. Catrina had been almost right about the name.

It took almost another hour before he sighted the spread, a medium-sized ranch, run-down looking, but with more cattle browsing the slopes than he would have expected given the general condition of fences and gates and the ranch buildings.

He saw a couple of distant riders hazing a small bunch of cows on some flats near a creek and two more sauntered out of the shade of the tumbledown bunkhouse as he rode into the yard. They were sloppy-looking cowhands, unshaven, crumpled clothes – but with thumbs hooked into gunbelts near their Colts. The one with the moustache and who was loose-limbed and looked lazy, spoke slowly.

'No work here, pardner.'

'Not looking for any.' Madigan folded his hands on the saddlehorn, waiting for the usual invitation to step down. It didn't come so he stayed put for now. 'Want to see Mrs Morton.'

'Why?'

'Private.'

The ranny smiled and shook his head emphatically. 'No. You gotta get past us if you want to see her and to do that you gotta tell us why, and Mitch an' me'll decide if—'

Madigan heeled the grey forward suddenly, catching them unawares. They jumped aside but he managed to kick the moustached one in the shoulder, staggering him.

The other swore, reached for his gun, but Madigan came out of the saddle with a rush and grabbed the man's gunhand, twisted the weapon from his grip and slammed him in the belly with it. The moustached one paused with his own gun half-drawn. He let it fall back into leather, rubbed at his tingling shoulder as he backed off.

'She's up at the house!' he gasped.

'Obliged. See to my horse, will you? I won't be long.'

The two cowboys watched as he walked easily up to the house, mounted the steps to the porch and raised a hand to knock. The door opened and Peggy Morton stood there, crookedly, as she leaned on a walking stick.

'I saw your meeting with Mitch and Long Tom. They mean well, but they get carried away a little. Come in.'

She was in her thirties, her hair a dullish red, paler than Haskell's had been. She looked tired, and coughed a little as she led the way into the parlour, leaning heavily on the stick.

'You must be Mr Madigan. Word has reached us out here about you.'

'I'm Madigan,' he confirmed, and accepted the glass of lemonade she offered. He drank it in a couple of gulps. 'Hot ride out here. . . .'

She eased herself into a chair and pointed to the

worn sofa for him to sit. He did so, balanced uncomfortably on the edge.

'What can I do for you, Mr Madigan? I must thank you for seeing that Carter – that was Red's real name – has had a decent burial and I believe you're arranging for a headstone?'

Madigan said he was and for a short time they discussed Red's saving Madigan from the Cheyenne and the lynching. She didn't seem unduly upset but she was disturbed.

'D'you think he murdered that woman?' Madigan asked bluntly.

'I don't know. Red was wild. His temper got him into a lot of scrapes. He liked women but I never heard of him mistreating them . . . but then we didn't see much of each other.' She fiddled with the handle of the walking stick. 'Red didn't approve of my husband . . . I don't know why. Just one of those cases where two people failed to hit it off. So he stayed away, but he did come to help me a few times after Will was killed. I was injured in the same accident.' Her blue eyes found his face. 'Our buckboard hit a rock and overturned . . . my broken leg never healed properly.'

'Sorry – must make things awkward for you.'

She smiled slowly. 'If that's a way of saying the place is run down, yes, you're right. It's hard for a lone woman to run a place out here, but Will made a lot of sacrifices to make our home and I felt it was my duty to carry on and do the best I could. . . .'

'I take my hat off to you, ma'am. Takes a lot of courage, and I wish you well. Anything at all you can tell me about Red? Specially the murder!'

She hesitated, tapped her work-worn fingers on the handle of the stick, glancing towards a cluttered bureau in one corner. Then she seemed to make up her mind.

'Red wrote to me after he broke out of jail. It's that letter in the dirty yellow envelope . . . some drifter delivered it one evening.'

Madigan rose, found the envelope and took it back to the woman. She signed for him to open it.

'I think I can trust you, Mr Madigan. You seem a genuine man and I'm grateful for what you're doing for Red's name.'

He sat down again and began to read. There was only one page of writing, a large, schoolboy scrawl.

Dear Sis:

I didn't kill her. She was alive when I left. Someone else must have done it. I'm on the run now but I won't always be. Got a couple things I need to check out, then you'll be OK. You can do all the things you ever wanted to do with the ranch.

I know I ain't much good, shoulda helped you more, but I'll do it proper soon.

> *Your brother,*
> *Carter (Red) Haskell*

Madigan reread the barely legible handwriting and then looked across at Peggy Morton. 'You know what he was referring to? These things he wanted to check?'

She shook her head and there was moistness in her eyes. 'No, I-I really wouldn't have any idea. It was just the thoughtfulness of him. There he was, on the run from the law, apparently for a crime he didn't even commit, and he – he was thinking of me and how he . . . could help me. . . .'

She tried to stifle the sobs but lost the battle, fumbled out a crumpled piece of lace and covered her eyes before wiping them and then blowing her nose.

'I'm sorry.'

'That's all right, ma'am. Like you say, it was mighty good of Red to be thinking of you in the midst of all his own troubles.'

'I'm afraid it hasn't helped you much.'

He stood, handing her back the letter. 'Wouldn't say that. Sounds as if Red knew something and that could even be the reason why they lynched him, didn't want to bring him to trial where he'd have his say in court.'

Her eyes widened. 'You make this sound a lot more sinister than it already is!'

'Well, it is, Mrs Morton. Someone tried to kill me on the way here. I'm going back to town now and find out for sure who it was. With a little luck, I might even figure out what Red was up to. I'll keep you posted, and I'm obliged for your hospitality.'

He was halfway to the door when she said, 'Not many folk know I'm Red's sister. Just who sent you to me, Mr Madigan?'

He turned. 'Catrina Harmon. You know her?'

Peggy Morton shook her head, frowning a little. 'No, I've never met her, but I've heard of her. Red mentioned her once. She's related to Judge Hannibal, I think he said . . . a niece or something.'

10
Death Trap

It was after dark when Madigan came within sight of the lights of Nightowl Creek. He was weary and dirty having covered the bodies of Carnaby and Reed with rocks near the waterhole. It wasn't much protection from the dog-coyotes he had heard howling at the sliver of new moon, but it would be something.

Likely Quinn would send someone out looking for them when they didn't return, anyway.

He was convinced now that Quinn would have sent those two: still not sure if Madigan *was* law or not, he wouldn't take any chances. Send the men who had a personal grudge against Madigan, then, if there was any trouble afterwards, he could always say it was just something that had to be settled privately. He would know nothing about it, of course. . . .

But there was something else he had to clear up before he went to brace Jackson Quinn – and maybe Judge Hannibal again, too.

He rode in through the backtrails and dark twisting narrow streets of the scattered shacks and cabins in the abandoned area of town. Madigan left the grey hitched to a sagging rail outside an empty barber's shop, unsheathed his rifle and levered a shell into the breech, afterwards lowering the hammer gently.

He made his way in the general direction of his own cabin but he was looking for the shack that Catrina Harmon had taken. It loomed darkly against the twinkling stars, easily recognizable by one corner where the drainpipe from the roof had rusted away and leaned out from the frame at an unsafe angle.

The place was in darkness, but he approached it quietly, walked around it warily, rifle hammer under his thumb. His injured shoulder was aching and there was dried blood halfway down his arm. No sound came from the shack. He tensed when someone laughed over on Main. There were still folk moving about there, doing last-minute shopping before the two general stores that were all that remained in the dying town closed up for the night.

She wasn't home. He stepped out from between Catrina's shack and the one next door and looked across at his own cabin. There was a dull glow showing through some of the cracks in the warped clapboards. *A candle* . . . so she was waiting for him there.

He moved across silently, paused at the door, lifting a boot ready to drive it against the old timber: he might be wrong and it might not be Catrina in there at all so he didn't aim to just walk in. Then he saw the old lidless trashcan lying on its side against the corner. OK, if there was someone hostile waiting, he might as well give them something to shoot at.

It meant leaning his rifle against the wall, but he did so and picked up the bin carefully, making as little noise as possible. Lifting it chest high, he balanced on one leg, kicked the door open and hurled the bin, at the same time palming up his sixgun.

There was a shattering roar, a flare of flame a foot long and suddenly the spinning can was hurled back into his face and he was knocked over backwards, dazed, nose and mouth bleeding, ears ringing, as he went down.

The roar tore through the ramshackle area and easily reached Main. Madigan shook his head, as he propped himself up on one elbow looking for his sixgun, blinking, not knowing what had happened.

Then in the light of the still sputtering candle inside the cabin, he saw the sawn-off shotgun tied to the back of a rickety chair, string leading from the trigger to the now sagging door. . . .

A death trap!

And he had almost walked into a charge of buckshot!

There were shouts and running feet as he was still struggling to get up, his ears ringing, head humming. He felt a couple of places on his upper right arm that were stinging and figured – correctly as it later proved – that a couple of the double-0 buckshot had hit him. *By God he had been lucky!*

He was half on his feet when rough hands helped him the rest of the way, held him while he steadied – and by that time Jackson Quinn had arrived.

As soon as he recognized Madigan, his sixgun came out and rammed against the dazed marshal's spine.

'I dunno what the hell you were tryin' to do this time, but you're just the man I want to see, Madigan. I'm arrestin' you for assault and hoss-stealing. Now grab two handfuls of air and march on down to the jail-house. We got a nice uncomfortable cell all ready and waitin'.'

The men who had first arrived were only too glad to help the sheriff and marched along with Madigan, crowding close, giving him no chance to make any fast moves. Folk were lining the walks now, staring without sympathy as he was taken to the law office.

Amongst the watchers, Madigan made out the slightly blurred shape of Judge Hannibal in his wheel-chair, a patterned Indian blanket wrapped around his legs.

The person pushing the wheelchair was Catrina Harmon. She stared soberly at Madigan, giving no sign at all of recognition.

'You missed,' he said, as he stumbled past.

'Next time,' she answered curtly.

Then he was shoved roughly into the law office and minutes later the door of his cell clanged shut.

They left him alone for a couple of hours and then, just as he was dozing off on the hard bunk, Quinn came up to the bars, holding a lantern.

'You son of a bitch! You killed Sel and Billy-Jack.'

Coming awake, Madigan forced himself to stay where he was, looked hard at the lawman.

'What was I s'posed to do? Stand still and let them bushwhack me?'

'Would've been easier all round,' Quinn admitted slowly. 'You've been one big pain in the butt since you arrived here, Madigan.'

'Glad to hear it.'

'Yeah, well, maybe you won't be so smart-ass with your comebacks from now on. We've had a bellyful of you. I still dunno whether you're a lawman or not, and it don't matter any longer . . . you're a hoss-thief and you assaulted the livery man, killed two townsmen who we damn well know you beat-up in the first place. There ain't no sympathy in this town for you.'

'Aw, hell, and for a while there, I thought I had an ally in Catrina.'

Quinn grinned tightly. 'Judge's niece. One tough lady. Was her idea to put on that act amongst them abandoned shacks. Got to you, din' she?'

'Very neatly. Set me up beautifuly for that ambush at the Indian well. Then just in case I made it she rigged the sawn-off in my old cabin. Yeah, I'd say she's pretty tough. So what're you gonna do with me now? Bring me to trial so the judge can sentence me?'

The sheriff shook his head slowly, lips pursed. 'Can't afford the risk. If you are law, someone'd be down here in two shakes with legal papers that'd put you back on the street again. You shoulda just let Red die out on the Plains, saved everyone a lot of trouble.'

'You gonna risk *two* lynchings?'

Quinn shrugged. 'Does seem like we'd be pushin' our luck. . . .'

Madigan nodded, looking hard at the lawman. 'Shot while trying to escape?'

'One option. Could put a well-known drunk in the same cell with you, feller who's been known to break a man's back when he's got a load of likker under his belt. Oh, don't you fret, Madigan, we'll think of somethin'. This town's ripe for anythin' and you're a threat, so you just make up your mind, you're never gonna see the inside of a courtroom.'

'Better hurry, Quinn, could be someone on their way to back me already.'

The sheriff stiffened. 'So!' He suddenly snapped his fingers. 'That damn letter to the Marshal's Office in Washington! You never did explain that away properly! You send for help? No, you couldn't't've. You'd only just arrived, had no idea what was goin' on. . . .'

'Maybe I was just bein' cautious.'

Quinn snorted. 'You? Not the way I see you. You're a goddam vigilante! You don't worry about back-up: you go in swingin' and bust heads, no matter whose they are. . . .'

Madigan sat up slowly, smiling. 'You got it right, Quinn. I don't care who it is: if they're in my way they either step aside or get stomped-on.'

Quinn curled a lip. 'You're just diggin' your grave deeper, Madigan!'

Madigan just smiled. Quinn frowned, started to speak, changed his mind, stared hard and long, then, with a muttered curse, he turned and strode away down the dark passage.

Madigan swung his legs over the side of his bunk,

dabbed at his oozing nostrils and the cuts on his face with his kerchief. He had set the cat among the pigeons, but trouble was, he had made himself the target.

He had shaken Quinn up some, but now he and his friends would have to move quickly, just in case Madigan had been speaking the truth about back-up coming.

It didn't give him much time, he figured, and wondered just how they planned to kill him. . . .

He was asleep when something dropped onto his chest and brought him wide awake instantly.

He clawed at the thing that had landed on him, half expecting to feel the clammy, scaly skin of a snake, but it was a slim, paper-wrapped object, no more than six inches long. Felt like a pencil. He jumped on to the bunk, grabbed the bars and pulled himself up to look out into the black alley behind the cell block.

It was too dark to see if anyone was there.

He eased down, opened the slim, pencil-like parcel and found he was holding a shiny surgical probe with a milled handle for a better grip. Madigan was surprised, unable to think for a moment, then he saw there was writing on the paper that had been wrapped around the probe.

He stood on the bunk to get some light on the words.

This will work on the door lock – at least it did for Red.
Use the side door, not the rear. You have to move fast.
They'll be coming soon.

Naturally it was unsigned but it was a woman's neat script. His first thought was that Catrina had written it, in another attempt to set him up, but there was just that touch – *at least it worked for Red.* He decided he would take the chance.

Hell, what real choice did he have?

It took longer than he expected, but he was able to use the slim-pointed probe to reach the edge of the tumbler in the lock and the steel withstood the pressure required to lift it. It went with a hard click and he pushed the door open fast and stepped out into the passage, pocketing both the note and the probe.

He needed weapons, but there was a light showing under the door at the end of the passage that led to the front office. *Damn!* He didn't know what he was stepping into, but he *had* to have something to protect himself with. . . .

He padded down to the connecting door, crouched and looked through the keyhole. There was no one behind the desk, just a lamp turned low. Maybe Quinn was consulting with the judge or his other cronies . . . or conveniently out of town again. Madigan took a chance and opened the door.

The office was empty, the street door closed but not locked. *Maybe they were working up another lynch mob in the saloon.*

He didn't speculate any more, quickly found his sixgun and rifle in a cupboard, strapped on his gun belt and hurried back into the cell block passage. He knew it was chancy taking the advice in the note about using the side door, but there was only that or the rear one and it was barred and padlocked.

So, no choice once again. He made sure there was a bullet in the rifle's breech, turned the handle silently, and then dived through, rifle at the ready.

Nothing happened and he felt pretty damn foolish as he somersaulted to his feet, crouching, swinging the rifle around looking for a target.

The night was warm and there wasn't much light from the stars and the new moon as he made his way warily towards the shed where the horses were kept.

Then someone stepped out of the shadows of the shed and he almost pulled the trigger as a voice said, 'Don't shoot, Mr Madigan! It's Marion Tucker!'

'So you were the one who helped Red escape.'

Madigan made it a statement not a question and Marion, eyes lowered, nodded jerkily.

They were in the small stables behind the infirmary now. Marion had led him there from the jailhouse, telling him she had a horse all saddled and provisioned for him. He was grateful, but there was a lot he needed to know before he decided to run.

'Yes,' she said quietly, in answer to his question, throwing a glance towards the darkened house and infirmary.

'Doc inside?' Madigan asked, and she nodded.

'Asleep, I guess – as usual. He's a . . . lot older than me. Has a lot less . . . energy. . . .' She spoke stiltedly and he had the impression she was about to make some sort of confession. He decided to help her out.

'You were having some kind of affair with Red?'

She snapped her head up. 'How did you. . . ? Oh, I suppose it's obvious enough now. Yes. Red and I used to meet whenever he was in town. There . . . there was no love involved. He just . . . just fulfilled a-a need that Doc couldn't. . . .'

'Doc know?'

'Oh, I think he knew there was someone. I don't think he knew it was Red Haskell.'

'And you got Red out of jail after they arrested him for Mandy Evans's murder.'

'Yes. There was lynch talk and I-I was fond of him. I knew he couldn't have done those terrible things to Mandy, even though he was infatuated with her . . . or perhaps because he was. . . .'

She just let her words trail off and the silence dragged while he waited for her to add more. But she didn't. She was very edgy and he knew she wouldn't stay much longer.

'Where does Catrina Harmon come into it?'

'Cat? That's what they call her. I don't know. She's a strange, vicious girl, goes away for long periods and then comes back to her uncle, the judge. She's more than half-man some say. In her ways, that is, not her looks.'

'Yeah, well, she tried to set me up for Reed and Carnaby to ambush. But back to Red. I've spoken with his sister and he wrote her a letter while he was on the dodge. Said he wanted to "check something" and afterwards his sister wouldn't have anything more to worry about. Sounded like a touch of blackmail to me.'

'I wouldn't know anything about that.' Marion spoke

quickly, nervously. 'I-I'd best be getting back inside.'

He put out a hand to her arm and restrained her, feeling her trying to pull away. 'Quinn and the judge are up to something. Maybe Doc's involved and you know about it and let something slip to Red. . . .'

Marion kept tugging at his arm, but he wouldn't ease up his grip. 'No! No I don't know anything. All right! I know they're up to something and Mandy Evans was somehow involved, but I swear I don't know what it is! *Please!* I have to go now. . . !'

'In a minute. Just tell me why you helped me get out of jail.'

She stopped her struggling, panting a little. 'I-I wasn't able to do anything to save Red when they came for him at the infirmary. It was awful. . . . The poor man nearly out of his head with pain after the amputation. . . . Oh, I – *please!* Let me go now! I just didn't want to be involved in another innocent man's death . . . or, perhaps "innocent" isn't the right word to use with you, Mr Madigan, but – I really do have to go!'

He released her. 'I'm obliged, Marion. You just stay quiet, don't get yourself into any trouble.'

But he was talking only to empty darkness.

He lifted the reins of the patient horse and led it out of the yard down towards the creek, splashed across and didn't mount until he was on the other side.

He didn't quite make it away from the town.

He was riding towards the western edge, not really having a destination, actually deciding if he would make a run for it or hide out somewhere in town.

Suddenly, a gun triggered two fast shots, but he

didn't hear any bullets and figured, even as he struck home with the spurs, that it was some kind of signal: someone had been watching the exits from the town – which either meant they knew already he had escaped, or it had all been a set-up, anyway, and he was about to be shot down as a fugitive.

Just as the horse under him gathered its muscles and leapt forward at the touch of the spurs, several voices shouted and there was a clatter of hoofs and a lot of splashing as waiting horsemen put their mounts across the creek.

Then the guns began to rip the night apart with their noise and muzzle flashes.

This time he heard the bullets.

The guns were being aimed at him.

11
Live Target

Marion gasped as she entered the dark bedroom in her house. A hand grabbed her by the upper arm, the fingers digging in deeply at the same time as she heard the gunfire down by the creek.

'You're arriving home late, my dear!' Doc Tucker's voice was hard-edged in the darkness, but even though it was dark, he flung her on to the bed, quite accurately.

By the time she had recovered, he had a lamp burning on the table. He stood over her. She frowned, fear knifing through her: she had never seen him look so angry.

'So! I can't imagine when it happened, but Madigan was yet another of your lovers, eh? You repaid him for his services, by letting him out of jail. Just as you did for Haskell!'

'You're mad!' She started to sit up but he pushed her down violently and this time the fear twisted within her. He had been angry with her at other times

113

over the years of their marriage but never like this. She lay sprawled on the bed, looking up at him with wide eyes.

Doc Tucker glared down at her. 'I could understand your philandering, Marion, and I don't really blame you for that, but you truly don't understand what you have done! You caused a near, total disaster by freeing that fool Haskell and now you've repeated the mistake by letting Madigan run free!'

'If I hadn't, what would've happened to him? Another lynching?'

'Oh, I think this time we might've been a little more subtle, but now, of course, it'll be the old "shot-while-trying-to-escape" excuse. Probably it will be accepted, but if it should turn out that he *is* a lawman . . . well, you can see my concern!'

She managed to struggle to a half-sitting position, frowning. 'No, I don't! I didn't know you were so involved in whatever it is you're mixed up in with Jackson Quinn and Judge Harmon, I thought you only—'

'See? Just as I was saying! You have no idea just what you have set in motion!' Suddenly he slapped her and the shock of the action more than the impact of his slim old hand made her gasp, as she put a hand quickly to her face. He leaned closer, his eyes burning. 'We will all be rich. The entire town! But Madigan can spoil our whole plan. He *has* to be stopped. Now, where has he gone? You *will* tell me, Marion. I'm very serious about this I assure you!'

'I don't know!' she shouted.

'But I think you could make a pretty good guess. . . .'
He turned and called, 'Now!'

The door opened and Catrina Harmon came in, her
face bright-eyed and alive with some kind of excite-
ment. She approached the bed smiling bleakly, then
brought her hand out from behind her back.

'You don't mind me borrowing these, do you, Doc?'
she asked.

Marion almost fainted when she recognized one of
her husband's scalpels and a pair of forceps.

Madigan wasn't sure where he was.

The night was black and he had twisted and turned
so many times that now he didn't have a direction he
could rely on. The town was out of sight so he knew he
had crossed the main ridge of mountains. He hadn't
been riding long enough for it to be the spur near the
Bowlegs, and if, as he thought, he was south of that
landmark, then his present trail might even take him
back past the town.

Quinn was no fool. The sheriff knew the country,
too, and if he figured Madigan might swing back in the
town's direction, he would have men waiting.

Even as he thought it out, Madigan swung the sweating, panting mount to the right, feeling the lift of the
ground almost immediately. They were on another
ridge slope. Glancing up he could see stars faintly
outlining the top, and glimpsed timber. So he was still a
long way from the trail he had taken that morning on
his way out to Peggy Morton's.

Quinn might even have men waiting at the Indian

well, but thanks to Marion Tucker, he would not have to
stop there. She had slung a large saddle canteen and a
smaller soldier's personal canteen on the saddlehorn
when she had prepared the horse. The animal itself was
a dark chestnut, even darker now with the streaming
sweat. It seemed a strong animal with good endurance.
He had a lot to thank Marion Tucker for – but would he
ever get the chance to do it? Not if that posse caught up
with him. Right from the start they had been shooting
to kill.

He swung left before reaching the top of the slope.
There was enough timber, he figured, for him to cross
without worrying about skylining himself. But maybe
Quinn would figure that was exactly what he would do
simply because it was easier.

So he swung down a ways, then stayed parallel with
the ridge top, urging the chestnut on when he felt the
ground dropping away beneath the hoofs. He rested
the mount a few moments, standing in the stirrups,
straining to hear above the animal's deep panting. *Yes!*
He definitely heard hoofs and the creak of saddle
leather below the trail he had been following originally.
The posse was heading upslope.

'Tag – take three men and get around to the other
side!' Quinn's voice startled Madigan and he instinctively tightened his grip on his rifle as the words drifted
across the slope. 'We'll catch him in a crossfire: and
shoot to kill! I've had enough of this pussy-footin'
around with Madigan! We'll haze him down to where
you are . . . you know the dry wash at the bottom that
leads to the Bowlegs?'

'We'll be there, Jackson!' a man answered, and he called three names and then Madigan heard the riders sliding their mounts back down the slope.

They rode across the grade away from him, but Quinn had given him a location now. He, too, knew the dry wash that led to the Bowleg spur: he had found it previously, before Reed and Carnaby had bushwhacked him.

But he wouldn't be using it this night.

And he wouldn't be setting himself up as a live target for these killers, either, if he could help it. Townsmen comprised the posse, of course, but they all seemed willing to shoot him on sight, which told him this thing, whatever the hell it was, was a lot bigger than he knew.

The whole damn town was involved!

He thought the clue was in that note Red Haskell had sent his sister. The piece about 'checking on something' . . . it seemed Red had learned something that had sealed his fate.

So, now that he had a rough idea of where he was and in which direction lay the Bowlegs, he figured his next stop had better be Peggy Morton's run-down spread.

But he didn't make it down the slope unseen.

Quinn had covered all possibilities, left three riders at the western end of the ridge, just in case Madigan did what he was doing now – avoiding the cross-over, coming down to the flats on this side of the ridge.

The first Madigan knew of them was the burst of gunfire that erupted from a brush-choked boulder field right at the bottom of the slope. He felt the horse lurch and its whinny was shrill as it swerved and broke stride, but quickly picked up when he touched its flanks with the spurs. It wasn't badly hit, he figured, when it put on a burst of speed, even as he straightened in the saddle and sent two fast shots back at the daggers of the muzzle flashes.

The men had chosen sandstone boulders and the rocks' lightness of colour gave away their positions as much as the muzzle flashes. They came thundering out of cover, shooting, and Madigan used his knees to control the chestnut, swerving it first left, then hurriedly right, hipping in leather as the rifle came up to his shoulder and he blew a man out of his saddle back there. That caused the other two to scatter wide, making him search for two targets instead of one.

Lead whispered past his ear, ripped the air close enough to his head to make his long hair jerk. He crouched low now, slid part-way to one side of the saddle, making an old Indian move that allowed him to shoot beneath the chestnut's arched neck. He only got off the one shot because the nearness of the rifle firing caused the animal to jerk and break stride, unseating Madigan. But even as he tumbled in the dust he glimpsed the man he had shot at being dragged behind his panicked mount, foot caught in the stirrup.

Madigan thrust to his feet, dazed, and the third man came in shooting and rode him down. It was like being hit by a runaway train, the impact taking him on the injured shoulder, spinning him wildly as his body hurtled through the air. He hit hard and rolled, losing the Winchester. The horseman wheeled and came thundering in again, lifting his rifle one-handed as the distance closed rapidly.

Madigan reacted by pure instinct. He palmed up his Colt and crouched as he fanned the hammer. There were only three shots – so fast they sounded like one prolonged roar – and the man twisted as he was lifted to his toes in the stirrups and collapsed to one side as the racing horse, frightened by the crash of the sixgun so near, swerved and threw the dead man completely out of the saddle. Madigan dived aside, the running horse just missing him.

But he was hurt, his left arm hanging uselessly, bleeding badly. And he only now realized a bullet had taken him just above the left hip, gone right through the flesh of his waist. He could hardly stand. His own horse had run off but stopped now, turning its head towards him, wide-eyed.

He recovered his rifle, reloaded the Colt awkwardly – he had little feeling in the fingers of his left hand – then staggered over to the chestnut and climbed clumsily into the saddle, wadding a kerchief over the bullet wound.

He heard the rest of the posse coming back down the slope at a reckless pace, turned the chestnut, and rammed home the spurs.

The night swallowed him up as he swayed in the saddle and hung on desperately with the reins wrapped about his wrists.

Madigan didn't know how he had found Peggy's Wildfire spread in the dark, disoriented as he was and with the pain in his arm and side blurring his vision.

But he came in from a north-westerly direction and saw the dark buildings spread before him. He was too desperate to take precautions he normally would, and rode in, right up to the house, dismounting with a clatter as he fell onto the porch. He dragged himself to the door and lifted a hand to rap on the panels but it opened and Peggy Morton stood there in a nightgown, leaning on her stick, a pistol in her other hand.

'Sorry to . . . trouble you . . . ma'am . . .' Madigan began and then he fell half across the stoop. . . .

When he came round he was on the sofa in the parlour and Peggy Morton was clearing away bloody rags and a bowl of rust-coloured water. He grunted as he tried to move.

'Just lie still,' she said quietly. 'You've lost a deal of blood and that arm has burst open the old wound. It doesn't look too good to me. You should see a doctor.'

'Long as it's not Doc Tucker,' he said breathlessly, and explained briefly what had happened. 'Marion didn't say so, but I think Doc's in this thing pretty deeply and she must've let something slip that aroused Red's suspicions.'

She was pale-faced and asked anxiously, 'How far is the posse behind you?'

'Don't know. Can't remember much after those three jumped me at the foot of the ridge. Didn't mean to lead 'em here.'

'That's all right. I'm glad you came to me for help – I think I'd better have Mitch take you to a safer place.'

'Mitch?' He rememberd the two lazy cowpokes who had greeted him last time he had been here. One had been called 'Mitch'.

'He's all right. Doesn't kill himself with work, but he'll help out. . . . There's a place where Red hid out for a little while. An old line shack, just north of here. I'll get Mitch to saddle you a fresh mount.'

'Thanks for your help, Peggy, but don't get yourself mixed up in this any more than you are. The posse comes and gets tough, you tell 'em the truth. Say I rode out if you like, but don't buy yourself more trouble.'

She half-smiled down at him. 'Red was my brother, Madigan. They lynched him. I don't owe those towns-folk anything. In fact, I feel it's the other way about. . . .'

The posse was closer behind Madigan than he had thought: Mitch hadn't returned from the line shack when they rode into the dark yard, clattering hoofs sending dust rising into the night.

Quinn stormed up to the house, followed by two armed men and pounded on the door, rattling the knob impatiently. It opened under his touch and he and his men had clumped into the parlour before a sleepy-eyed Peggy Morton entered with her cane and her pistol.

A light flared as one of the posse men lit the lamp and gave a start of surprise. 'Sheriff Quinn! What on earth are you. . . ?'

'No time for pussyfootin' around, Peggy,' Quinn snapped, sweaty and dirt-glazed and in an impatient mood. 'We're after Bronco Madigan.'

'Who is Bronco Madigan?' Peggy asked.

'Damnit, I just told you, no time for any fancy foot-work, here!' Quinn snapped. 'We want to know where Madigan is.'

Already she could hear more of the sheriff's men stomping through the house and she knew they would have also wakened the cowhands in the bunkhouse.

'I don't know any Madigan—'

Quinn surprised her by grabbing her by the shoulders, lifting her easily off the floor and depositing her roughly on to the sofa. He leaned down towards her.

'Peggy, we know he saw you earlier today! He's wanted for murder and hoss-stealin', and he broke out of jail. He's on the run, killed at least three of my men. . . .'

She was still denying that she knew Madigan when a man came in from the kitchen with a bowl that showed traces of blood around the rim and he said there were fresh bloody rags in the stove, not yet burned.

Peggy didn't have to say anything. The door opened and Catrina Harmon came in, hair wild, a narrow-brimmed hat hanging down her back by a rawhide thong around her slim neck. Her eyes were bright as Quinn asked, 'What're you doin' here?'

Catrina kept her eyes on Peggy Morton. 'Had a talk with Marion Tucker in town. She seems to think Madigan might've been making for here.'

'He's been here,' Sheriff Quinn told her, tight-lipped. 'Frank found rags and stuff. He's hurt but we don't know where he is right now. . . .'

Catrina smiled, still watching Peggy. 'Go find something to do outside, Jackson, I'll have a talk with Peggy. You know – woman to woman. I'm sure she'll see it's best to tell us what we want to know. . . .'

Quinn gave her a hard stare, then, clamping his jaws together, nodded jerkily, signing for his men to follow him as he left the room. Catrina propped a chair under the door handle.

'What d'you think you're doing?' demanded Peggy, getting to her feet, leaning heavily on her walking stick.

Catrina crossed swiftly, kicked the stick away and Peggy gasped as she fell, just catching the sofa and saving herself from sprawling on the floor. Catrina grabbed her roughly and flung her on the sofa.

'Stay there!' she snapped, reaching into her jacket.

'I will not!' Peggy snapped angrily, struggling up. But she stopped abruptly as Catrina brought a small canvas-wrapped package from her pocket and casually unrolled it.

It contained two scalpels, forceps, surgical needles. . . .

Peggy's face lost all its colour as she sagged back on the sofa.

Quinn and his men were gathered in a tight bunch, smoking and talking quietly in the yard when the door opened and Catrina stepped out on to the porch. She seemed a little breathless and there was the sheen of sweat on her face.

The men looked at her silently, uneasy in her presence: they had all heard the screams coming from the parlour.

'He's in some ruins to the south-west,' the girl told Quinn. 'An old stage station, she said it was ... might be one of her men with him.'

'I know the place,' Quinn snapped. 'C'mon, men – let's go get this chore done.'

Catrina watched them mount and ride out and then went back into the parlour where Peggy lay, white-faced, blood on her clothes, holding a cloth over a bleeding hand. She was shaking and looked sick.

'Why did you send him off in the opposite direction?' she asked, her voice strained.

Catrina smiled, picking up her blood-stained instruments. 'I have a private thing to settle with Madigan, you see. Twice I failed to kill him or have him killed, I don't intend for there to be a third failure. So this time I'm going to see to it myself.'

She reached down and pulled Peggy Morton to her feet where the woman swayed.

'And I'm going to take you along so you can watch, Peggy dear. I think you'll like it ... I know I will.'

'You're ... sick!'

Catrina laughed. 'Not as sick as Madigan's going to be.'

12
Pow-wow

The line camp had been abandoned for many years and was falling down. The roof was mostly open to the sky. The one large room was filled with rubble from the shingles and rotted supports, collapsed furniture. But there was one fairly substantial bunk and Mitch helped Madigan on to this, afterwards going outside and cutting some brush to stuff into a burlap sack to use as a mattress.

Madigan had his guns with him as well as the grubsack and warbag and the canteens.

'Obliged, Mitch. You'd best get back to Wildfire. Mrs Morton might need your backing.'

He looked steadily at the cowpoke, his eyes glazed a little with pain, but still making Mitch uncomfortable.

'I ain't much with a gun, mister.'

'You work for her, you give her what loyalty you can and that takes in whatever talents you've got.'

Mitch moved his feet across the gritty floor. He had lit a candle stuck in the neck of an empty bottle and the flickering light showed Madigan that the man couldn't meet his gaze.

'I weren't hired on to do no fightin',' Mitch mumbled.

'You ride for the brand, you fight for the brand – goes without saying. Didn't anyone teach you that?'

Mitch sniffed and shrugged.

'Put it this way, Mitch: I get over this and I find out anything's happened to Mrs Morton because you wouldn't back her, I'll come looking for you.'

The cowboy flushed. 'No need to get tough – it's just that I-I ain't one for trouble.'

Madigan made an exasperated sound. 'We could go round on this all night – you get on back and you do like I say.'

Mitch straightened and curled a lip. 'I don't take no orders from you.'

'Just this once, try it.'

'Aah, you don't mean nothin' to me!' And Mitch turned abruptly and went out. Madigan heard him ride off and was relieved that the sounds were of one horse only. Whether Mitch had put Madigan's mount out of sight he didn't know . . . he hoped so, because he didn't want anyone to find him here like this: weak from blood loss, left arm about useless. . . .

In the middle of the thought he passed out.

When he opened his eyes, the candle had burned more than halfway down – and there were two people in the ruined cabin.

He struggled to sit up and the rifle fell off the edge

of the bunk. A blurred shape appeared beside him and kicked the rifle underneath, then lifted his sixgun from his holster and tossed it into a corner.

By that time his vision had cleared enough for him to recognize Catrina Harmon and, behind her, looking weak and sick, one hand heavily bandaged, Peggy Morton leaning against a wall. Even as he watched she slid down slowly to the floor.

'I'm sorry, Madigan,' she gasped. 'I-I'm not very brave. . . .' She held up the bandaged hand, the cloth stained with blood. 'She cut off the first joint of my little finger.'

That brought Madigan back to full consciousness and he forgot about his pain as he looked into the smiling, beautiful face of Catrina.

'You sadistic bitch!'

She laughed and placed a hand in the middle of his face, shoving him back roughly. He moaned involuntarily. She took out the scalpel from her pocket, turned it so the light glinted from the blade.

'I can be very . . . persuasive when I want to be. Like Peggy said, she's not very brave. . . .'

'You mean it was over too quickly for you, didn't give you a chance to work up a thrill from working on her slowly. I guess it was you who did the cutting on Mandy Evans.'

Catrina's eyes narrowed, then she nodded. 'We had to shock the town, get them involved, turn their hate in one direction so they'd lynch Red Haskell. Once they did that, we had them. The whole town felt guilty, you see?'

Yeah. But not guilty enough: they were still greedy.

'Yeah, I see, but Marion Tucker spoiled it by setting him free. Then I obligingly brought him back for you. Who is it, Cat? You?' Quinn, the judge. . . ?'

'I just told you, it's the whole town now.'

'*What* is?'

She laughed. 'You don't need to know. But what I need to know is if you really are a lawman or not.' She slashed with the scalpel, the blade slicing air scarcely an inch from his face as he jerked back. She laughed again. 'Don't worry, Madigan. I won't cut you up – not just yet.' She turned abruptly and strode to where Peggy Morton sat against the wall. She pulled the woman to her feet by her hair, pushed her back with one hand, held the scalpel threateningly in front of her face as she looked over her shoulder at Madigan. 'I'll work on Peggy for now . . . unless you want to be a spoil-sport and tell me right away.'

He squirmed into a more comfortable position on the bunk, grunting, sweat standing out on his gaunt face. 'Leave her alone. Yes, I'm a US Marshal.'

Catrina sobered. '*Federal* law! Mmm – we didn't expect that. So it looks like we have to set up something special for you. . . . You're going to have to die in such a way that it can't be blamed on the town. But, just in case you're trying to be smart, I think I'll do a little carving on Peggy while you try to convince me you're telling the truth.'

Madigan tensed, easing around again in the bunk, trying to get a comfortable position.

'Leave her be!' he snapped. 'I'm speaking gospel. I

work out of Washington, and my boss is Chief Marshal Miles Parminter. I've been working in Montana and—'

Then his right hand came up from beside him and something flashed briefly in the flickering candlelight and Catrina rose to her toes, gasping sharply. The sharp steel probe that Marion had given Madigan to use on the cell-door lock protruded a few inches from just under her ribs and she clawed at it, face going white as the shock surged through her slim body.

Then she bared her teeth and lifted the scalpel, preparing to slash Peggy Morton's throat.

Madigan tumbled out of bed, snatching the rifle from under the bunk and firing it one-handed. The heavy slug at that range took Catrina between her breasts and lifted her clear of the ground, throwing her across the room to sprawl on a pile of rotting shingles. Dust rose about her as she arched her back and slid off, rolling on to her face, the scalpel falling from her slack fingers. . . .

Peggy Morton had covered her face with her hands and now looked through spread fingers as Madigan floundered on the floor, gasping, grimacing in pain. The bandage around his side was wet with spreading blood and the woman made a small sound, got to her feet and limped across to him.

Madigan was in plenty of pain as Peggy Morton helped him back into the bunk. He was breathing hard, sagged back, vision blurred, body throbbing. She tore at the bandage, saw the blood flowing and opened the package of bandages and medicines she had packed for him. She wadded cloth and held it over the wound. He lay there, grey-faced, staring up at the stars through the ragged hole in the roof.

'Quinn . . ?' he managed to gasp.

'I don't know where he is. Catrina sent him and the posse to the south where the ruins of an old stage station are. She wanted you all to herself.' She changed the rag. 'Oh, this bleeding just won't stop!'

'When could Quinn get . . . back here?'

She didn't answer at first, busy with the wound. Then she straightened a little, one hand still holding a wad of cloth against the open wound. She used the other hand to brush a wisp of hair back off her face.

'I'm not sure he knows where you are, but we passed Mitch going back to the ranch on our way up here. If Quinn goes there he'll soon have it out of him.'

'How soon?'

'I don't know. Maybe he won't get back much before daylight. Then he'd have to come here.'

'Patch me up as best you can and we'll get moving.'

'Good heavens! You can't be moved! You've ripped that wound wide open! You try to sit a saddle and it'll never stop bleeding.'

'We can't stay here.' Madigan's voice was weaker now and the sweat was running down his face and body. 'I don't trust Mitch; he'll tell everything as soon as Quinn asks. What's to the north?'

She frowned. 'Nothing in the way of settlements. The Union Pacific railroad is laying a line up there but they only have temporary camps. Anyway, there's been a lot of trouble with Indians attacking their camps and sabotaging the rail line. They claim Union Pacific is laying track over sacred country . . . it's too dangerous to go that way.'

Impatiently, Madigan waved a hand. 'Where else then? There's got to be somewhere. . . .'

She stared at him, seeing he was determined to move no matter what. 'There's rough country all around. The nearest town of any size is Elk Mountain on the river, but getting there would be very hard. . . .'

'Shove a handful of bandage in that wound and let's get moving. We stay here, we're both dead.'

She worked fast over the wound, turned a puzzled face towards him. 'Just what is happening, Madigan? People being murdered; Catrina – she's always had a reputation for being vicious, but I-I'd never seen her like she was at my place. . . .'

'Never mind the talk. I dunno what's going on, but we'll never find out if we don't get out of here.'

Peggy bound him up as tight as she dared – he needed to be able to breathe although each time his ribcage moved he winced. She took time to cover Catrina's body with some of the shingles and he could see she was in pain from her own hand.

It was sheer hell mounting his horse but somehow she managed to help him into the saddle and he instructed her to rope him in. She did so expertly and by that time there was just the beginning of a line of pale grey in the east.

Before they were ready to pull out, Madigan shook his head to clear his vision a little, looked down from the narrow bench where the line shack stood. He thought he could make out movement at the edge of dark timber, perhaps the first of the posse. . . .

'We can't get down from here,' he grated, gesturing when she glanced at him sharply. 'If that's the posse, they'll see us coming off the ridge . . . we'll have to go up.'

'That's north – I told you there's nothing there but the railroad construction camps.'

'Maybe we can make one of them. Let's go, Peggy! For *Chris'sakes*, let's go – *now!*'

It was daylight by the time the weary posse reached the abandoned line camp.

They found Catrina's horse tied to a bush outside and the woman's body inside. Jackson Quinn kicked a heap of shingles savagely.

'Stupid bitch! Too damn keen to use a knife. Sent us on a wild goose chase just so she could have her fun with Madigan and Peggy Morton. Now see what it got her!'

He scowled down at the dead woman, looked around him a little wildly. The other men in the room stifled yawns, swaying on their feet with fatigue. They had been riding all night and many of them were fed up with the chase.

Chuck Burdette, one of the two remaining store-keepers in Nightowl Creek spoke for a lot of men when he said, 'Jackson, there's blood everywhere on that bunk. Mitch said Madigan was bad hit – he can't ride far like that. My guess is he'll bleed to death, so I reckon we oughta head back to town – or you can split us up, some go on if you've a mind, the rest of us go home.'

Several men crowding into the shack supported the suggestion. The sheriff scowled.

'Bunch of old daisies! It's almost certain now Madigan's law of some kind. We've got to shut his mouth for good, and the only way we can do that is to catch up with the sonuver! All right, quit your bitchin'! Get outside and look for tracks. They din' come down from the ridge so they must've gone up and over. So let's get after 'em.'

No one seemed very keen and there was a lot of complaining, loudly and under their breath. It made no difference: Quinn was determined and they mounted wearily, even their horses protesting, as they kicked them on to the steep, winding trail leading up and over the ridge and into the mountains. Splashes of blood showed them the way, also the scrabbling hoof-prints left by the fugitives' horses in the soft earth.

Quinn was out ahead, mighty anxious to catch up with Madigan. The woman was an extra problem, but by now the townsmen ought to be ready to tackle that without too much bitching. Not that it mattered – she *had* to die with Madigan. No telling how much she knew and that was one of the most tantalizing things: he didn't know how much *Madigan* knew, either. Whether he was here officially or, as he claimed, just rode in accidentally after being jumped by that war party of Cheyenne renegades. Could be, of course – the whole country was crawling with them now that the army was tied-up to the north, bands of them hitting settlers, even the UP railroad. *Now fancy that!* he chuckled. *Wonder why?*

There was a good-sized bounty on Black Star's head now: the railroad would gladly double it, anything to keep the Indians from hitting them, lousing-up their schedule.

Quinn laughed quietly, shaking his head, but the townsman riding alongside heard and snapped his head around.

'What's so funny, Jackson? I don't see nothin' funny in this!'

'Got no sense of humour,' was all Quinn would say, his voice rough from too many cigarettes and from being too long in the saddle without proper sleep. 'Just keep goin' and we'll all be laughin' soon enough.'

'You and the judge been sayin' that long enough!'

'Just hang an' rattle a mite longer, Jude, just hang an' rattle. You'll be glad you did.'

Jude scowled and dropped back alongside Chuck Burdette. 'I've about had a bellyful of this, Chuck.'

'Me too – so've most of the boys. We'll tag along a little longer, but there ain't no sign of Madigan and the woman by noon, I'm cuttin' out an' headin' for home.'

'I'll come with you!'

But the fugitives were sighted an hour before noon: they were next mountain over and climbing slowly, their horses obviously feeling the strain. Through the field-glasses, Quinn could plainly see Madigan sagging in the saddle, only the ropes holding him on the horse.

'Come on!' Quinn said. 'We can catch up with 'em before they top-out on that mountain! Let's go!'

No one was enthusiastic, but there was some energy

in the response: one final effort and they could have the chore over and be back in town just after sundown, they figured. . . .

They were wrong.

Oh, they gained ground, all right, on the struggling fugitives, set their own trail-burned broncs down the slope into the ravine between the mountains and started up the second slope, lashing and spurring their horses cruelly.

Peggy Morton saw or heard them and dropped back and leaned from her saddle, trying to lash Madigan's mount to greater speed. But the animal was near exhausted and Madigan was lolling loosely, obviously unconscious.

Quinn bared his teeth in a tight grin of triumph.

'We've got 'em! We've got 'em cold!'

Then the Indians appeared.

Painted, whooping, shooting; they surged out of the timber and the boulders and charged the posse.

Quinn and his men were caught flat-footed and two men reeled in the saddle and a third crashed to the ground as the Cheyennes' gunfire swept their ranks.

Quinn had his rifle out and working, yelling at the others to scatter. But the order was unnecessary: the men were spread out all over the slope, going hell-for-leather down into the ravine. Some horses stumbled and one man clung wildly to his mount's mane, running alongside, his legs going out from under him finally and he fell. An Indian bullet took him between the shoulderblades

The posse were forced to come together, pinching in

as they entered the narrow ravine. Quinn was swift to organize them into a tight group, concentrating the fire on the whooping renegades. The posse's volley tore into the Indian ranks and several fell, a couple more lurched in their saddles. Quinn whooped and hollered at the success of the manoeuvre and he had some of the men dismount and kneel, the others, still in their saddles, shooting over their heads, concentrating their fire.

Now that the tables had been turned, the Indian leader, Black Star, held up his hand and wheeled his mount across the face of the slope, still shooting at the posse, but making away from the ravine, heading back into the mountains. His band followed with posse lead singing about them.

The white men cheered as they hastily reloaded, the short but savage battle having set their blood racing.

'All right!' Quinn bawled in his rough voice. 'That's it! Let 'em go. Ain't nothin' to be gained by chasin' 'em . . . son of a bitch shouldn't been attackin' us anyway.'

'We whipped their asses, Jackson!' panted Jude, eyes wide.

'Mebbe, or mebbe that's only Black Star's way of lurin' us after him—'

'Jackson!' said Chuck Burdette, pointing. 'There's Black Star! Settin' his pony atop that rock, plain as you like.'

'Don't shoot!' snapped Quinn, as rifles rose to shoulders. He took off his hat and waved it in an arc, nudging his mount forward. 'Cover me.'

'Judas, man, you ain't goin' out there!'

'Just cover me. First thing that looks queer, you blow him outa the saddle.'

The sheriff spurred his mount forward and up out of the ravine, across the face of the slope to where Black Star still sat his mount atop the flat rock ledge. Quinn stopped below, back out where he could see the Indian clearly, his rifle ready in his hands.

'The hell you doin' attackin' me and my men, Black Star?'

'Not recognize you, Quinn. Thought you white men looking for my camp.'

Quinn smiled crookedly. 'So! We're somewheres near your hideout, eh! Well, don't worry, we ain't after you.' Quinn pointed up the slope. 'There's a man and a woman goin' up an' over the next ridge ... they've caused me a lot of trouble. Your men want to try out their new guns, they can kill 'em both. Do me a favour.'

Black Star's face, almost unreadable because of the black paint, seemed carved from granite as he stared down at Quinn. 'I do favour – what I get?'

Quinn shook his head slowly. 'Hell, the pleasure of killin' a coupla whites. One's a woman, not a bad looker, you and your men can have some fun. The man, well, you can kill him slowly, long as you kill him.' He squinted up at the Cheyenne. 'You do this for me, Black Star, and I won't forget it, I promise.'

Black Star grunted: it could have meant anything. He wheeled his mount and rode off, disappearing amongst the rocks.

Quinn rode back to his curious men.

'C'mon, boys, we can head back home now.' They

stared at him, in disbelief – yet pleased, too. Quinn smiled crookedly. 'How much chance you reckon Madigan and the woman have of makin' it over the mountain now?'

They grinned and Chuck Burdette said, 'Yeah! Let the Injuns do the job for us! You hear that, boys? We're headin' home!'

As they rode across the ravine to the far mountain, Quinn half-hipped in the saddle and looked back. He couldn't see the slopes where Madigan and Peggy were, but he was confident the Cheyenne would kill them both eventually.

And that would be as good a way as any for Madigan to die, whatever kind of lawman he was.

Let the Cheyenne take the blame. . . .

13
Vigilante Law

The light was queer. There was a strange smell, too, a little like rancid neat's-foot oil, but pleasant enough in its own way. He had smelled it before but couldn't recall where at the moment.

The light was coming through his closed eyelids and he was surprised that he was having to make an effort to actually open his eyes. He felt weak, drained. He was aching and had a couple of really sore places, too: his left shoulder and upper arm and, further down on the same side, just above his hip. His first thought was that he had been trampled by a horse, but he couldn't remember breaking-in any mustangs recently.

In fact, he couldn't recall anything much at all that had happened to him recently.

Instinct made him lie as still as possible, breathing shallowly, gathering his senses that seemed mighty dulled. He knew somehow that it was dangerous for him not to have an edge on his situation: maybe *deadly* dangerous.

That was when the memories began to flow back . . . the attack by the Cheyenne war party on the Great Plains, Red Haskell's rescue and then the on-flowing events after he had reached Nightowl Creek, ending with the escape from the line camp. Then the dizzying slopes of the mountain and Peggy's alarm at seeing the posse closing in. He passed out about that time, coming halfway back to consciousness for a few moments to hear Peggy scream, sounding terrified:

'*Oh, my God! It's Black Star!*'

At that point he opened his eyes and found he was lying on a pile of buffalo robes inside a sunlit teepee. Which explained the smell of hides and the strange light. He saw the bow and arrows in the buckskin quiver dangling against one sloping wall, a shield with a black star painted on it. He couldn't twist his head any further and grunted with the effort.

The sound brought someone to kneel beside him. A fat Indian woman with braided hair and porcupine-quill necklace with a blue stone and two feathers at the middle. Her hand was gentle against his forehead and she said something quietly in her own language. He knew a little Cheyenne but didn't catch her words. She moved away and soon after Peggy Morton limped in, using her stick, and stood at the foot of his bed of hides, looking down at him. She smiled, and he noticed she was wearing a buckskin dress.

'Thank goodness, you're coming out of your fever! I've been worried for days.'

When he spoke his voice was raspy, his throat dry.

'Days? I've been out to it for that long?'

'In a fever.' She went to a pottery jar with a ladle in it, scooped out some water a little awkwardly because of her injured hand, and leaned down to hold it against his scaly lips. He drank greedily but she had only brought him a little. 'More later. . . . How do you feel?'

'Getting clearer-headed, but I'm damn sore.'

'No wonder. You burst both wounds open at the line camp, saving me from Catrina.' He nodded, remembering now. 'Moon Woman and her friends have packed your wounds with herbs and I must say they're achieving faster healing than any medicine I know of.'

'We're in the Cheyenne camp?'

'Yes. A war party led by Black Star attacked the posse but were driven off. They found us and I think they would've killed us except Black Star recognized you. He said you were too brave to die any other way than in battle, so he would make you better and one day you two might meet again and – fight to the death.'

Madigan nodded slowly. 'Some Indians are like that. Where is he?'

Peggy looked a little alarmed, glanced around, then moved closer, speaking softly. 'I understand Cheyenne fairly well – my husband did a lot of trading with them before Black Star stirred some of them up to break out of the reservations. I haven't let on that I know most of what they're saying. Black Star has led a party to the north to attack the Union Pacific rail camps. They're planning on derailing a supply train, too. . . .'

'Must be something to do with this "sacred ground" they claim the railroad is crossing. Otherwise I guess there's not much they could hope to get from those temporary railhead camps.'

Peggy hesitated. 'I think there's something else behind it, but I can't quite pick it up.'

'What d'you mean? "Something else". . . ?'

'I'm not sure. I think they're doing it – oh, I don't know, really. It might be just that I'm not really fluent in Cheyenne. A lot of it I can put together by simple logic but some. . . .' She shrugged.

Madigan was puzzled too but he was very weak still and found himself drifting off into sleep even as she spoke.

When he woke again it was dark and he was hungry. Moon Woman was there and brought him an elk stew which he ate and some roasted corn cakes which gave his jaw muscles a work-out. He was somewhat amazed when she brought him coffee to wash it down. But when she showed him the bag the beans had come from, he really wasn't surprised when he saw the UPRR lettering on the cloth. So Black Star and his men were taking the provisions from the railroad camps they raided. The so-called trespassing on sacred ground could be just an excuse to raid the construction camps for whatever loot they could lay their hands on.

It was three days before he saw Black Star. The muscled warrior came in silently and stood looking down at Madigan who was now propped up on his bed of buffalo hides.

'You better soon.'

'Heading that way – I'm obliged, Black Star.'

The Indian grunted and Madigan noticed he was holding a new-looking Winchester and had a bandoleer of cartridges slung across his chest.

'You get better, you go, woman stay.'

Madigan tensed. 'Why?'

'You don't tell where camp is then.'

'No, Black Star, I won't tell, but she comes with me when I go.'

Black Star shook his head. 'You come back for her when you strong. Then we fight.'

'I don't want to fight you. The woman comes with me.'

The Indian frowned. '*Your* woman?' Madigan hesitated, nodded. 'She lame!'

The marshal forced a smile. 'She's a good woman and she must come with me.'

'Or mebbe you both stay!' the Indian said thoughtfully.

Madigan sighed. 'Look, Black Star, I give you my word I won't tell anyone where your camp is. We both have to leave together. We have enemies we must fight.'

'Ah! Quinn.'

'How did you. . . ?' The Cheyenne said nothing and Madigan gestured at the rifle. 'Present for raiding the railroad?'

Black Star almost smiled. 'Yes – *for* raiding.'

Somone was giving the Indians guns to hassle the Union Pacific. Why?

'Railroad cross sacred ground,' Black Star said, as if he had read Madigan's mind. 'The pass you call Sara-to-ga we know as Way To Spirit World. Caves where holy men buried there. No good for white man to go that place.'

'Well, I guess you have a point. Why not tell Union Pacific? Or Guv'ment?'

Black Star spat: it was sufficient comment, brought about no doubt from previous dealings with the whites.

'Better my way. OK, Mad-i-gan. When you better, you go and take woman. Next time we meet, we have good fight.'

Madigan smiled thinly. 'Guess there's no way out of it – you going to use that new rifle on me?'

Black Star looked surprised, held up the gun. 'This for railroad.' He patted the knife at his waist in a fringed buckskin sheath. 'This for you. Great Spirit happy if I send you to him.'

'Happier than I'd be,' murmured Madigan, but said aloud, 'I hope we never cross trails again. I don't want to kill you.'

Black Star smiled. 'You don't worry. I kill *you!*'

Madigan never could figure the Indian way of thinking so left it at that and a few days later when he was hobbling about the camp on a stick, he noticed that most of the guns that the warriors had were new-looking. Certainly better weapons and more of them than when he was attacked and Red had thundered in with shotgun and Winchester blazing. They wouldn't have withdrawn so quickly if they had been armed as they were now.

He had been right – someone *was* running guns. There was no other way the Cheyenne could've come by them: the railroad camps wouldn't have big stocks of new Winchesters.

*

It was another seven days before Madigan and Peggy Morton left the Cheyenne camp. Black Star and his men were away somewhere – likely raiding the railroad again – and Madigan, still not certain that Black Star was going to let him go without wanting to fight him, woke Peggy in the night, motioned for her to be silent. They slipped away from the sleeping camp, the horses watched only by a youth who had fallen asleep on the job.

They led their horses away silently and mounted only when they were far down the dark slope.

'Where the hell are we, anyway?' Madigan asked. 'I've been looking around during the day and far as I can figure we're somewhere in the Medicine Bows.'

'I think so. I was too terrified when they picked us up to take much notice, but we started off the way we'd been travelling and I'm pretty sure we kept mostly to that direction – until the last few miles, then we went towards the west. The sun was starting to set so I'm sure about that.'

That gave Madigan something to work on but he wished he had his guns: the Cheyenne had kept them.

But no Indians came after them and they found their way back to Peggy's Wildfire spread. Madigan was surprised at how well he was standing up to the long trail ride. The Indian herbs had worked wonders.

Mitch and the others had ransacked the place of everything of value that could be sold for a few dollars, leaving only a little food. Cattle were still grazing on the range but they had taken the horses from the corrals.

Peggy led him to her bedroom and opened the clothes closet, lifted the floorboards and showed him an Ithaca shotgun and a Colt in a dusty leather holster with cartridge belt.

'These were my husband's. He wasn't a violent man, never used the guns except for hunting ... I don't know if they still work. ...'

But Madigan had them working within thirty minutes. 'I'm going into town. It'll be best if you stay here, Peggy.'

'Yes. I want to start clearing up this mess left by Mitch and his friends. What're you going to do?'

He smiled crookedly. 'Throw a little surprise party – for the whole damn town. ...'

Sheriff Jackson Quinn strode past Judge Hannibal's hard-eyed manservant, Leon, and made his way to the parlour. The judge was in his wheelchair, Indian blanket around his legs, his haggard face drawn and hatchet-like. He glanced up as the lawman entered and Leon stood in the doorway awaiting orders. Judge Hannibal signalled for the man to leave them and Leon closed the door quietly.

'Havin' trouble with Doc Tucker, Judge,' the sheriff said without preamble. 'Says he can't contribute no more money to buy more guns for Black Star.'

Hannibal frowned. 'Damnit! It'll only take one or two more raids and then Union Pacific will *have* to decide which way they're going – due west through Saratoga Pass, with guaranteed Indian trouble, or swing south towards Nightowl Creek, where we'll be waiting to welcome them. I don't see that they'll have much choice.'

'I know – I reckon we oughta get the Injuns to blow the pass down and then UP would just have to divert through this way.'

'Sealing off the pass is a good idea but you'd never get the Indians to do it. They really do regard it as sacred. Lucky I read-up on the local tribe or we wouldn't have a chance of rejuvenating the town. No, it'll have to be one final massive raid on the railroad camp – and it'll have to be done before the army gets around to sending soldiers to give them protection. We've been lucky so far.'

'Well, Black Star'll only take payment in guns – and, Judge, I ain't sure it'll be safe round here with all them new rifles in the hands of them Injuns.'

'We have to take that chance if we want the railroad here. I guess I'll have to pay for another shipment of rifles.' He rolled the chair across to a desk and unlocked a drawer, pulling it partially open. 'But this will be the last. And I'd feel a whole lot better if I knew for sure that Madigan was dead.'

Quinn scowled. 'Ah, he's dead, all right. The Injuns would've took care of him a coupla weeks ago.'

Hannibal frowned. 'I hope so.'

'Take my word for it, he's coyote food by now.'

'Wrong, Quinn – I gave 'em indigestion.'

The double doors leading out to a small balcony crashed open and Madigan strode in, holding the shotgun, covering both startled men. Hannibal clawed at his chest, his face turning grey with the shock.

Quinn, too, was startled, but he recovered quickly and reached for his sixgun. Madigan cracked the Ithaca's barrels across the sheriff's wrist. The gun slid back into leather as Quinn clutched his bleeding hand against him.

The other door was kicked open and Leon came charging in, sixgun in his right hand blazing as soon as he saw Madigan.

The marshal dropped to one knee, triggered, the shotgun filling the room with thunder. Leon, running forward, stopped as if he had hit a wall, spun into the splintered doorframe and staggered back, before pitching out into the passage where he fell to the floor on his face.

Madigan stood, covering Quinn and the judge who was gasping for air, clawing at his leg blanket, bringing out a small vial of amber liquid. His hands shook violently as he removed the cork and tossed the medicine down his throat. He shuddered, jaw trembling, eyes staring.

'I *told* you you should have checked with that Indian to make sure he was dead!' Hannibal's voice was shaky and weak but his anger was still evident as he glared at Quinn.

'You *oughta* be dead, you son of a bitch!' the sheriff said to Madigan.

'Better men than you've tried to kill me, Quinn. So, you've been using Black Star to give Union Pacific a bad time before they reach Saratoga Pass? At that point they either have to continue laying track due west or swing south, because there just isn't any other way for them to go, to get around the Medicine Bows. And that would bring the railroad through this dump, and turn it into a boom town overnight. Not a bad idea.' Madigan's voice suddenly hardened. 'Trouble is, I'm here to see it never happens.'

'You could never prove we bought guns for those Indian renegades,' growled Quinn, tying a kerchief around his hand now.

'He's right, Madigan,' agreed the judge. 'You may have worked it out, but where's your proof, man?'

Madigan nodded. 'Yes, Judge, *proof* – that's what's been bothering me. And how you got access to new Winchesters.'

'Oh, Mandy arranged that. On one of her visits to the East she met a certain colonel who was married to a general's daughter. A little seduction, a little blackmail and we had several fake orders for shipments of Winchesters. Then Jackson here made arrangements with Black Star. . . .'

'Why kill Mandy?'

The judge was wheezing as he spoke and his face tightened at Madigan's question. 'Well, that was Catrina's doing.'

'Just who the hell was she, anyway?'

'A very strange woman, but my niece. There was some trouble back East and the family sent her out to me. Not a good idea, but she did have – certain uses. Unfortunately, she set her sights on Red Haskell who, even though something of a ladies' man, was not prepared for Catrina and her – aberrations. And Cat never could take rejection. Because of Red's infatuation with Mandy it made Cat very jealous, and when she saw Red leaving Mandy's place that night and went in and found her unconscious she . . . she killed Mandy, made it look like Red had murdered her and suggested we set it up for a lynching. . . .'

'Which involved the whole town and gave you a hold over them. Yeah, I know all that. Catrina told me.'

The judge gave a death's-head smile. 'But with Catrina dead, too, you are still lacking proof, Madigan.'

'Yeah,' the marshal agreed slowly. 'I don't have a scrap of proof that would stand up in court, but I do have something else.'

Both Quinn and the judge looked puzzled.

'What?' asked the sheriff sceptically.

Madigan smiled bleakly. '*I* know what's happened.'

He let that sink in and the judge shook his head. 'Knowing is simply not enough, Madigan.'

'It is for me. A court might throw out my story, but *I'd* still know the truth, so. . . .' He looked from one man to another. 'Looks like I'm just going to have to be judge and jury myself.'

The judge started to shake again, his face grey. 'Wh-what d'you mean?' His hands began to jerk and one eyelid drooped, his jaw pulling to one side.

'Just what I said, Judge. Sometimes vigilante law is the only law that works. I'm finding it out the hard way, but there you are. . . .'

'You–you're mad! You–you're a duly sworn lawman! You can't do that!'

'Watch me.'

But he ought to have been watching Hannibal more closely. Because the judge was exhibiting signs of an incipient stroke, Madigan hadn't paid as much attention to him as he should have.

Now the judge reached in under his leg blanket but this time did not draw out a vial of medicine, he brought out a .44 calibre derringer and it cracked, the ball striking the barrel of the shotgun, jarring it out of Madigan's hands.

Quinn yelled and jumped to one side, snatching at his gun with his bruised hand. Madigan dropped to the floor as he palmed up his sixgun rolling to one side. Quinn's first bullet splintered the floorboards beside him and then the marshal triggered and Quinn spun away. Madigan swung the gun as Judge Hannibal brought up the derringer again and he shot the judge through his thin chest, the impact sending the wheelchair rolling back to jar against the wall.

Then he twisted back towards Quinn who was down on one knee trying to bring up his gun for one last shot at Madigan. He never made it. Madigan's bullet took him through the neck and Jackson Quinn twisted away, crashing on to his face, twitching for a few minutes before becoming still forever.

The judge was still alive, though, wheezing, coughing blood, the derringer having fallen from his scrawny hand now. He stared up at Madigan with dulling eyes.

'The whole town was in on this deal, Judge, so the whole town's going to pay. . . . We'll start right here.'

Madigan picked up the desk lamp, smashed it on the floor beneath the sofa. It blazed up in seconds and by that time he had the other two lamps smashed against the drapes and one wall. The place was lit up by the flames like a corner of Hell and Judge Hannibal reached out a clawing hand as Madigan brushed by, pulled the money sack from the open desk drawer, then scooped up the shotgun. He kept on going, past the sagging judge, stepping over Leon's body in the hallway, on his way out. Already the weathered clapboards were ablaze, the roaring of the flames filling the night.

He made his way down into the town and set fire to the abandoned part, the old buildings flaring up almost instantly, crackling and exploding as dried-out fibres heated up. The fire spread towards the occupied part of town, and halfway down Main, he shot out a window of one of the stores and tossed a bundle of blazing rags inside.

Folk were streaming out into the streets, panicking, calling for water, others shocked, watching in horror as their own dwellings were caught in the conflagration.

A couple of men shot at Madigan, but a charge from the shotgun had them diving for cover, forgetting about trying to stop him: dousing the flames was more urgent.

In the saloon alley, two men tried to jump Madigan. He dropped to one knee as lead whined off the wall and a charge from the Ithaca picked up one man and hurled him back. The other just stood there, shocked, and Madigan clubbed him to the ground. More men yelled at him, but a couple of shots over their heads and they ducked back into the bar. It gave him time to fire up the pile of old crates stacked against the rear wall of the saloon. It was a roaring torch by the time he discovered the man he had knocked down was Mitch. He kicked the man to his feet.

'Where's Peggy's horses? Talk quick, you son of a bitch, or I'll throw you in the fire!'

Mitch was scared white as he saw Long Tom lying bleeding almost at his feet. 'We . . . we sold 'em to Swede. . . .'

'You go cut 'em out of the corrals and get 'em down to those willows on the creekbank and wait for me – I have to come looking for you, I'll blow your damn head off!'

Mitch nodded shakily and made for the corrals behind the livery while Madigan, reloading the shotgun, walked into the stables.

Swede was trying to get his horses out of the stalls and, when he saw Madigan, the livery man grabbed for a rifle. Madigan drew his Colt and put a bullet through his arm without breaking stride. He grabbed the man by the shirt front and slammed him against the wall.

'I'm taking back Mrs Morton's horses and I expect you to help drive 'em out to her spread. Meantime, let's get these animals out of danger.'

Clutching his bleeding arm. Swede staggered around, freeing the horses in the stalls. Madigan lent a hand, saw them off safely into the night and told Swede to go help Mitch. 'You be waiting with Mitch when I get back or I'll find you and kill you, Swede!'

The livery man nodded staring in awe at the marshal.

Then Madigan made his way to Doc Tucker's infirmary.

Marion met him on the porch, pale and dishevelled, her face swollen and bruised. She had been crying.

'You're too late. Once he saw the fire, Doc knew you were back. He took poison. . . .' She covered her face with her hands. 'It was horrible!'

Madigan squeezed her shoulder. 'Likely the best way, Marion. Look, I'm driving some horses back to Peggy Morton's place shortly. You'd best come with me. Go get some things together and I'll meet you back here. You'll be better staying with Peggy for a while.'

She nodded numbly, still crying, as she turned back into the house.

Madigan walked on, preparing to set fire to the next block but stopped, watching the scene before him.

Flames leapt twenty feet high into the night. Half the town was ablaze. The people were desperately trying to save the other half and also to put out the fires that were already destroying the business section of Nightowl Creek.

Maybe it was enough, he figured.

Maybe this was sufficient payment for what they had done to Red Haskell . . . and the railroad construction workers who had died in Black Star's raids. Justice had been served.

Madigan's kind of justice.

He found McCann, the stonemason, standing in his gateway, staring at the fires. He glanced at Madigan's face reflected in the ruddy light.

'You?'

Madigan nodded. 'That headstone finished yet?'

'Yes. This afternoon. I had Ernie set it up on the

grave. Quinn actually did have the body moved to a better part of the cemetery, you know.'

'Yeah – he was worried about me at that time. Before he decided it would be safer if I was dead. How's the hand?'

McCann held up the bandaged hand. 'I think I'll be able to use it again. It'll take time, of course.'

Madigan paid him some money and then walked out to Boot Hill. There was a better view of the fire from here, but he was no longer interested in it. And the townsfolk were too busy to be interested in him any longer. There was enough red light reflected from the ruddy sky to show him the headstone standing firm and upright on Red Haskell's grave. It read:

Red Haskell
Died a Hero Saving the Life
of a Grateful
Bronco Madigan, US Marshal

'Thanks, Red— Hope you rest easy now.'

Madigan touched two fingers to the brim of his hat before he turned away and walked back to where he had tethered his mount. He would drive the horses back to Peggy Morton's spread with Marion Tucker, stay a while and help get the place into some kind of order.

He would have to do something about Black Star, stop his raids on the Union Pacific. Maybe Parminter could use his influence, have some soldiers sent down right away to help protect the railroad workers. Then round-up Black Star's renegades and send them back to the reservation. . . .

There would be punishments, of course, but there was nothing he could do about that. It was the old story – white man and red man. He would keep his word: he wouldn't give away the location of Black Star's camp, but that was as far as he could go. Respect for Cheyenne culture didn't allow for the on-going massacre of whites who were just going about their everyday jobs.

And he knew that if he and Black Star ever *did* meet again it would be one *helluva* fight . . . and it would mean death for one of them.

And *he* would be in trouble with Miles Parminter, too, but likely not for long. The chief marshal would find another chore for him.

There was always another chore waiting.

Always.